KT-438-572

## HOW I SURVIVED BULLIES, BROCCOLI, AND SNAKE HILL
(with Chris Tebbetts)

I'm excited for a fun summer at camp—until I find out it's a summer *school* camp. There's no fun and games here, I have a bunk mate called Booger Eater (it's pretty self-explanatory), and we're up against the kids from the "Cool Cabin" . . . there's gonna be a whole lotta trouble!

## ULTIMATE SHOWDOWN
(with Julia Bergen)

Who would have thought that we—Rafe and Georgia—would ever agree on anything? That's right—we're writing a book together. Discover: Who has the best advice on BULLIES? Who's got all the right DANCE MOVES? Who's the cleverest Khatchadorian in town? And the best part? We want you to be part of the fun too!

## SAVE RAFE!
(with Chris Tebbetts)

I'm in worse trouble than ever! I need to survive a gut-bustingly impossible outdoor excursion so I can return to school next year. Watch me as I become "buddies" with the scariest girl on the planet, raft down the rapids on a deadly river, and ultimately learn the most important lesson of my life.

# THe
# I FUNNY
## SERIES

## I FUNNY
### (with Chris Grabenstein)
Join Jamie Grimm at middle school where he's on an
unforgettable mission to win the Planet's Funniest Kid
Comic Contest. Dealing with the school bully (who he
also happens to live with) and coping with a disability
are no trouble for Jamie when he has laughter on
his side.

## I EVEN FUNNIER
### (with Chris Grabenstein)
Jamie's one step closer to achieving his dream!
This time, be amazed as he fends off the attention
of thousands of star-struck girls, watch in awe as he
reduces the school bully to a quivering mess, and join
the masses as he becomes the most popular kid in
school. Or something like that . . .

## I TOTALLY FUNNIEST
### (with Chris Grabenstein)
Jamie's heading to Hollywood for his biggest challenge
yet. There's only the small matter of the national finals
and eight other laugh-a-minute competitors between
him and the trophy—oh, and a hurricane!

KT-438-572

## HOW I SURVIVED BULLIES, BROCCOLI, AND SNAKE HILL

(with Chris Tebbetts)

I'm excited for a fun summer at camp—until I find out it's a summer *school* camp. There's no fun and games here, I have a bunk mate called Booger Eater (it's pretty self-explanatory), and we're up against the kids from the "Cool Cabin" . . . there's gonna be a whole lotta trouble!

## ULTIMATE SHOWDOWN

(with Julia Bergen)

Who would have thought that we—Rafe and Georgia—would ever agree on anything? That's right—we're writing a book together. Discover: Who has the best advice on BULLIES? Who's got all the right DANCE MOVES? Who's the cleverest Khatchadorian in town? And the best part? We want you to be part of the fun too!

## SAVE RAFE!

(with Chris Tebbetts)

I'm in worse trouble than ever! I need to survive a gut-bustingly impossible outdoor excursion so I can return to school next year. Watch me as I become "buddies" with the scariest girl on the planet, raft down the rapids on a deadly river, and ultimately learn the most important lesson of my life.

# The
# I FUNNY
## SERIES

### I FUNNY
(with Chris Grabenstein)
Join Jamie Grimm at middle school where he's on an unforgettable mission to win the Planet's Funniest Kid Comic Contest. Dealing with the school bully (who he also happens to live with) and coping with a disability are no trouble for Jamie when he has laughter on his side.

### I EVEN FUNNIER
(with Chris Grabenstein)
Jamie's one step closer to achieving his dream! This time, be amazed as he fends off the attention of thousands of star-struck girls, watch in awe as he reduces the school bully to a quivering mess, and join the masses as he becomes the most popular kid in school. Or something like that . . .

### I TOTALLY FUNNIEST
(with Chris Grabenstein)
Jamie's heading to Hollywood for his biggest challenge yet. There's only the small matter of the national finals and eight other laugh-a-minute competitors between him and the trophy—oh, and a hurricane!

2 420283 21

**DAD**
He's kind of kooky, but he draws cool ninja comics.

**SAMMY**
That's me!

**MOM**
For a genius, she sure invents some dopey robots!

**DRONE MALONE**
For traffic reports or spy jobs, he's your robot.

**MADDIE**
The coolest sister in the whole world— I mean it!

**MR. MOPPENSHINE**
He attacks dust until it cries for help!

**HAYSEED**
His green thumb is actually painted aluminum.

**BLITZEN**
This former robo-linebacker is now a really aggressive lawn mower.

**E**
Hmm...I can't think of *anything* he's good for.

These robots do everything in my high-tech home, from making breakfast to handing out toilet paper. Wanna see how I ended up with a whole gang of gizmos?
**COME ON IN!**

# Also by James Patterson

## THE WORST YEARS OF MY LIFE
(with Chris Tebbetts)

This is the insane story of my first year at middle school,
when I, Rafe Khatchadorian, took on a real-life bear (sort
of), sold my soul to the school bully, and fell for the most
popular girl in school. Come join me, if you dare . . .

## GET ME OUT OF HERE!
(with Chris Tebbetts)

We've moved to the big city, where I'm going to a super-
fancy art school. The first project is to create something
based on our exciting lives. But I have a BIG problem: my
life is TOTALLY BORING. It's time for Operation
Get a Life.

## MY BROTHER IS A BIG, FAT LIAR
(with Lisa Papademetriou)

So you've heard all about my big brother, Rafe, and now
it's time to set the record straight. I'm NOTHING like my
brother. (Almost) EVERYTHING he says is a Big Fat Lie.
And my book is 100 times better than Rafe's. I'm Georgia,
and it's time for some payback . . . Khatchadorian style.

# The
# TREASURE HUNTERS
## SERIES

## TREASURE HUNTERS
### (with Chris Grabenstein)

The Kidds are not your normal family, traveling the world on crazy adventures to recover lost treasure. But when their parents disappear, Bick and his brothers and sisters are thrown into the biggest (and most dangerous) treasure hunt of their lives. Evil pirates, tough guys and gangsters stand in their way, but can they work together to find mom and dad?

## TREASURE HUNTERS:
## DANGER DOWN THE NILE
### (with Chris Grabenstein)

The hunt continues, and this time the Kidds are taking on the hair-raising dangers of the Nile. They meet some seriously BAD guys along the way, risking life and limb to find the legendary mines of King Solomon . . . and their mom and dad, of course!

Kenny Wright is a kid with a secret identity. In his mind, he's Stainlezz Steel, super-powered defender of the weak. In reality, he's a chess club member and a "Grandma's Boy". Kenny wants to bring a little more Steel to the real world, but can he stand up to the bullies at school?

# HOUSE OF ROBOTS

## JAMES PATTERSON
### AND CHRIS GRABENSTEIN

**ILLUSTRATED BY JULIANA NEUFELD**

5 7 9 10 8 6

Young Arrow
20 Vauxhall Bridge Road
London SW1V 2SA

Young Arrow is part of the Penguin Random House group of companies
whose addresses can be found at global.penguinrandomhouse.com

Copyright © James Patterson 2014
Illustrations by Juliana Neufeld
Excerpt from *Middle School: Just My Rotten Luck*
copyright © James Patterson 2015
Illustrations in excerpt from
*Middle School: Just My Rotten Luck* by Laura Park

James Patterson has asserted his right to be identified as the author of this
Work in accordance with the Copyright, Designs and Patents Act 1988

First published by Young Arrow in 2014
First published in paperback by Young Arrow in 2015

www.randomhouse.co.uk

A CIP catalogue record for this book is
available from the British Library

ISBN 9780099568285

Printed and bound by Clays Ltd, St Ives Plc

Penguin Random House is committed to a sustainable future
for our business, our readers and our planet. This book is made
from Forest Stewardship Council® certified paper

*For my mom.*
*—C.G.*

*To India—*
*for ten amazing years at Palm Beach Day Academy.*
*And for Andrea Spooner—my hero.*
*—J.P.*

| RENFREWSHIRE COUNCIL | |
|---|---|
| 242028321 | |
| Bertrams | 03/05/2017 |
| | £6.99 |
| BOW | |

# CHAPTER 1

Hi, I'm Sammy Hayes-Rodriguez. Maybe you've heard of me? I'm the kid everybody's making fun of because my mother made me bring a robot to school with me—the dumbest, most embarrassing thing to ever happen to any kid in the whole history of school. (I'm talking about going back to the Pilgrims and Mayflower Elementary.)

I need to tell you a wild and crazy story about this robot that—I kid you not—thinks it's my brother.

And guess where the dumb-bot got that goofy idea?

From my mother!

Hi, I'm SAMMY'S FRIEND TRIP. I'M NOT EVEN IN THIS CHAPTER, BUT HERE I AM ANYWAY.

Oh, guess what? My father is in on this idiotic robot business, too. He even called Mom's lame-o idea "brilliant."

BEST IDEA YOU'VE EVER HAD, LIZ. ABSOLUTELY GENIUS!

NINJA ROBOTS!

Good thing Maddie is still on my side.

Maddie's absolutely the best little sister anybody could ever have. Aren't her blue eyes incredible? Oh, right. *Duh.* That drawing is in black-and-white. Well, trust me—her eyes are bluer than that Blizzard

Blue crayon in the jumbo sixty-four-color box.

Anyway, Maddie and I talked about Mom's latest screwy scheme over breakfast, which, of course, was served by one of Mom's many wacky inventions: the Breakfastinator.

MADDIE

Punch the button for Cap'n Crunch and cereal tumbles into a bowl, which slides down to the banana slicer, shuffles off to the milk squirter, scoots over to the sugar sprinkler, and zips down to the dispenser window.

Want some OJ with your cereal? Bop the orange button.

But—and this is super important—do NOT push the orange juice and Cap'n Crunch buttons at the same time. Trust me. It's even worse if you push Cap'n Crunch and scrambled eggs.

Maddie and I always have breakfast together before I head off to school. The two of us talk about everything, even though Maddie's two years younger than I am. That means she'd be in the third grade— if she went to school, which she doesn't.

I'll explain later. Promise.

Maddie knows how crazy Mom and Dad can be sometimes. But to be honest, even though she's

younger, Maddie keeps things under control *way* better than I do.

"Everything will be okay, Sammy. Promise."

"But you totally agree that Mom's new idea is ridiculous, right? I could die of embarrassment!"

"I hope not," says Maddie. "I'd miss you. Big-time. And yeah, her plan is a little out there...."

"Maddie, it's so far 'out there' it might as well be on Mars with that robot rover. They could dig up red rocks together!"

Okay, now here's the worst part: My mom told me that this wacko thing she wants me to do is all part of her "most important experiment ever."

Yep. I'm just Mom's poor little guinea pig. She probably put lettuce leaves in my lunch box.

MUST... CATCH... CHEESE!

# CHAPTER 2

**M**om's "Take a Robot to School Day" idea is so super nutty, she couldn't even say it out loud in front of Genna Zagoren, a girl in my class who has a peanut allergy, which is why my best buddy, Trip, can never eat his lunch at Genna's table. More about Trip later, too. Promise.

Anyhow, it's time to begin Mom's big, *super-important* experiment: me and a walking, talking trash can going to school. Together.

"Just pretend he's your brother" is what my mom says.

"I don't have a brother."

"You do now."

Can you believe this? I can't.

As for the robot? I don't think he's really going to blend in with the other kids in my class except, maybe, on Halloween.

He's already wearing his costume.

"Good morning, Samuel," E says when we're out the front door and on our way up the block to the bus stop. "Lovely weather for matriculating."

"Huh?"

"To matriculate. To enroll or be enrolled in an institution of learning, especially a college or university."

I duck my head and hope nobody can tell it's me walking beside Robo-nerd.

GREAT. MOM'S SENDING ME TO SCHOOL WITH C-3PO.

"We're not going to college," I mumble. "It's just school."

"Excellent. Fabulous. Peachy."

I guess Mom is still working on E's word search program. I can hear all sorts of things whirring as the big bulky thing kind of glides up the sidewalk. The robot chugs his arms back and forth like he's cross-country skiing up the concrete in super-slow motion. Without skis.

I notice that E is lugging an even bigger backpack than I am.

Maybe that's where he keeps his spare batteries.

According to my mother—whose name is Elizabeth—the robot's name, E, stands for *Egghead*, which is what a lot of people call my mom, Professor Elizabeth Hayes, PhD, because she's so super smart (except when she does super-*dumb* stuff like making me take a talking robot to school for anything besides show-and-tell).

My dad, Noah Rodriguez, says the name E stands for *Einstein Jr.* because the robot is such a genius. Ha! Would a genius go to school without wearing underpants? I don't think so.

My sister, Maddie, thinks E is a perfect name all by itself and stands for nothing except *E*.

I kind of like Maddie's idea. Even though Maddie

doesn't go to school, she's so smart it's almost impossible to fight or argue with her about anything. Trust me. I've tried.

But the more time I spend with E, the more I think I know what his name really means: *ERROR!*

"Remember, Samuel," E says when we reach the bus stop, "always wait for the school bus on the sidewalk. Do not stand, run, or play in the street."

A lot of my friends from the neighborhood are already at the corner. Most of them are gawking at the clunky machine with the glowing blue eyeballs that's following behind me like an obedient Saint Bernard.

"What's with the bright blue eyeballs?" I mumble. "Are those like freeze-ray guns?"

"Let's form a straight line, children, away from the street," E chirps. And get this—E can smile. And blink. (But you can hear the mini-motors clicking and purring inside his head when he does.)

"I make these suggestions," E continues, "in an attempt to enhance your school-bus-boarding safety."

Everybody stops gawking at E and starts staring at me.

None of the kids are smiling. Or blinking.

E is definitely the biggest ERROR my mother has ever made—worse than the time she designed a litter-box-cleaning robot that flung clumps of kitty poop all over the house.

"What *is* that thing?" asks Jackson Rehder, one of the kids who ride the bus with me every morning.

"Another one of my mother's ridiculous robots," I say, giving E the stink eye.

"What's his name?"

"E. For *Error*. Just like in baseball."

"I'm sorry, Samuel," says E. "You are mistaken. You are imparting incorrect information. Your statement is fallacious."

Great. Now the stupid robot wants to argue with me? Unbelievable.

Stick around. This should be fun.

# CHAPTER 4

"I am sorry, Samuel. *Error* is an absurd name for a technologically advanced machine that is able to sense, think, and act on its own."

"Then go *be* on your own and leave me and my friends alone!"

"I am sorry, Samuel. I have been programmed to attend school. It is my primary function."

"Well, go attend one where I'm not a student."

"I am sorry, Samuel—"

"Hey, Sammy," cracks Jackson, "maybe that's his name: *Sorry*! He sure says 'I'm sorry' a lot."

E rotates his head thirty degrees to the left, tilts down, and locks in on Jackson Rehder's eyes. "I am sorry, Jackson. My name is E. Your suggestion is totally illogical. For one thing, the word *sorry* does not begin with the letter *e*."

E swivels back to face me.

"I must go to school with you, Samuel. It is what Mother told me to do."

"Mom?"

"Professor Elizabeth Hayes, PhD."

"I know Mom's name! And she's not your mother, she's *mine*!"

E actually grins. "Of course Elizabeth is my mother. Perhaps not in the limited way you look at the world, Samuel. But most certainly Professor Elizabeth Hayes, PhD, is my creator and, therefore, my mother."

"So the robot *is* your brother?" snaps Jackson. "He's your robo-bro? Your bro-bot?"

Everybody at the bus stop picks up on that: "Robo-bro! Ha! Bro-bot!"

What a great start for "Error" and me, huh? I'm

beginning to think I might actually hate this thing.

Finally, the big yellow school bus comes rumbling down the street, and I happily realize that there's no way E will be coming to school with me today.

Robots can't climb steps, right? They roll around on tank treads or bounce off walls. Well, you have to scale three giant steps to board the school bus. Something E won't be able to do.

You're going *down*, Bot Boy!

**CHAPTER 5**

"Once we are safely on board the bus," E peeps as the driver swings open the folding doors to reveal the steep little staircase, "go directly to a seat and remain seated and facing forward for the entire ride."

"*Riiiight,*" I say, hopping up the three steps lickety-split.

When I reach the little landing at the top, I spin around to wave buh-bye to E, who will be spending the rest of his day stranded on the sidewalk, totally ruining his shot at a perfect-attendance medal on his very first day of school.

"See ya...wouldn't want to be ya!"

Yes. I am gloating. Just a little.

But the robot has the last laugh. Well, he doesn't actually laugh, because I think Mom forgot to give the thing a sense of humor.

What E *does* do (I hate to admit) is pretty amazing.

He lifts one foot and places it on the first step and—*CLICK, CLUNK, CLICK, CLUNK, CLICK*—he climbs up those steps faster than I can.

"Why have you not taken your seat, Samuel?" E asks, because I'm standing there with my mouth hanging open, blocking the aisle.

"Yeah, little dude," says Mr. Hessler, the school bus driver. "Sit down."

The door closes. The air brakes make a gassy noise as if they've been eating bean burritos all morning.

Yep. I'm on my way to school.

And E is coming with me.

Did I mention that I might hate this thing?

Well, I decided that I do.

I really, *really* do.

CHAPTER
6

I don't want to be obnoxious here or brag...but guess who was absolutely *right* about E going to school being a huge mistake? A colossal ERROR?

Yep. It was me. Sammy Hayes-Rodriguez.

Day one of Mom's experiment is a total bust, just as I predicted it would be.

My reward for being so smart?

A chance to take part in the *first-ever* parent-student-teacher-robot conference in the principal's office.

Since our house in the Sunnymede section of South Bend, Indiana, is all of nine minutes away from Creekside Elementary (and because our hybrid is equipped with an enhanced GPS Mom designed that picks the quickest route by somehow communicating with all the stoplights along the way), both Mom and Dad were able to attend the cozy little conference.

I couldn't wait for Mrs. Reyes, our school principal, to expel E—forever.

It's not Mom's fault, really. Some experiments just don't work out. Like that mad scientist in the old movie who ended up as a human fly. Major fail.

"I am so, so sorry about the...incidents," my mom says to Mrs. Reyes, who's pretty cool most of the time, but if you ask me, she's way too lenient with

my mother. Maybe that's because they play together in a terrible rock band. (More on that later.)

"I completely support Elizabeth," says my dad. "And Sammy. And Einstein Jr. And you, of course, Principal Reyes. In short, I support everyone and, uh, every*thing* in this room."

"I made a minor miscalculation," my mom continues. "Or two. Maybe three. Might've been four."

Mrs. Reyes smiles. Nods thoughtfully. It's what principals do.

"These things happen, Elizabeth," she says. "Especially when you're trying to boldly go where no one has gone before in your quest for knowledge."

See what I mean? *Way* too lenient.

"But," says Mrs. Reyes, standing up and taking a deep breath, "we will get through this, just as we get through each and every exciting day here at Creekside."

While Mom and Dad and Mrs. Reyes are all saying good-bye and shaking hands, E and I have a "moment" together out in the hallway.

"I wish you could have been a bit more supportive of me on my first day of school," says E.

If I didn't know he was a robot, I'd swear he was kind of choking up.

"Frankly, Samuel, I felt a little lost. Discombobulated. Confused. Flummoxed. Who wouldn't? After all, it was my first day. And I am so different from all the other boys and girls."

Okay.

Now I'm feeling pretty bummed, too.

CHAPTER
7

**W**hoa. Wait a second.

Before everybody, including me, starts getting all weepy about E being suspended on his first day of school, let me tell you *why* Mom was apologizing for Error.

No. Hang on. Let me tell you why my mother should've been apologizing to *me* instead of the principal.

Let's do a quick recap of what happened *before* that little parent-student-teacher-robot conference.

Okay—the second we arrived at school, Error caused a near riot.

"Greetings and salutations to you all!"

(That's E. Not me.)

I'm just shaking my head, wishing I could disappear—but that's extremely hard to do when you're walking up the halls with a five-foot-tall, whirring, clicking, knobby-kneed plastic guy with bright blue LED eyeballs.

"Is that a robot in our school?" asks this one kid.

"No. It's a knight in shining armor," I snap back.

"Is that a robot?" asks a girl.

"No. It's an action figure from my life-sized *Star Wars* collection."

Before anybody else can ask the same stupid question, Cooper Elliot, probably my worst enemy in the known universe, breezes up the corridor and jumps in my face.

"Hey, Dweebiac."

Yes. That's what Cooper Elliot calls me. Constantly.

"I see you brought a friend to school. Smart move. You needed one."

"He's not my friend," I say, moving as far away from E as I can, which isn't very far because Cooper kind of has me boxed in.

Now the big doofus gets right in my grill. "C-3PO here isn't your friend?"

"No. He's one of my mother's dumb experiments."

"Oh. So he's just like you? Because—face it, Sammy—you were your mother's dumbest experiment *ever*!"

"Excuse me," says E, lightly tapping Cooper Elliot on the shoulder with one of his clamps, which are supposed to be like hands. "Was that a joke? If so, I will proceed to chuckle amusedly."

"No," says Cooper, pulling back a little. "The only joke I see is you, you overgrown can of creamed corn. You and Dweebiac."

"Actually, my brother's name is *Samuel*, not Dweebiac."

For half a second, it feels pretty good to have RoboCop sticking up for me like that. I mean, his vise-grip clamper-claws are powered by high-pressure hydraulics. E could crush a coconut between his pincers. Or Cooper Elliot's nose.

"Your *brother*? Oh, man. That is priceless!" Cooper has to hold his sides, he's laughing so hard. "Dweebiac is your brother?"

"Affirmative. But as I stated previously, his proper name is Samuel."

"Hey, you guys, guess what?" Cooper booms to the

whole hallway. "Dweebiac's brother is a robot! The two of them are BRO-BOTS!"

Remember that good feeling I mentioned? It's gone.

Especially after everybody else starts piling on, saying stuff about E. And me.

None of it is very nice.

SO WHAT DO YOU GET WHEN YOU CROSS A ROBOT AND A TRACTOR?
A TRANS-FARMER!
WHAT DOES A ROBOT EAT WITH HIS HOT DOG?
SILICON CHIPS!
HEY, ROBOT, RUST IN PEACE!
ROBOTS FOR DUMBOS
CLICK
WERE WE INVADED BY ALIENS LAST NIGHT?
HOW COME NO ONE TOLD ME?!
STRANGEST-LOOKING SUBSTITUTE TEACHER EVER.

## CHAPTER 8

**O**f course, those semi-predictable, early-morning insults were not what the first-ever parent-teacher-student-robot conference was all about.

You got a minute for this? Good. I'll give you the blow-by-blow.

Okay. E and I finally made it to Mrs. Kunkel's classroom. She wanted to start the day going over spelling and grammar. E? He wanted to start by showing off.

"Shall I spell *Kyrgyzstan*?" he asks with his hand shot straight in the air.

"Um, it's not on our vocabulary list this week," says Mrs. Kunkel.

"How about *cantaloupe*? *Dirigible*? *Enormous*?"

"Like your eyeballs?" cracks Cooper Elliot.

Mrs. Kunkel gives Cooper a look. "Let's move on to grammar...."

And again E pipes up. "Personal pronouns—such as *I*, *we*, *they*, *he* or *she*—take the place of specific nouns."

"That's right," says Mrs. Kunkel. "But in the future, E, please wait until I call on you."

"*You* is also a pronoun. *You and I* is correct, if the words are used as subject pronouns. *You and me* is correct when they are used as object pronouns."

And it gets worse. Much, much worse.

E starts picking up steam. Literally. I see puffs of white smoke coming out of his earholes.

It goes on like this through math, social studies, and even phys ed, where E creates this huge scene by using our gym teacher, Coach Stringer—who weighs about two hundred and fifty pounds—as his human dumbbell.

The next, shall we say, "incident" takes place during lunch in the cafeteria.

Bobby Hatfield throws a tangerine at Tom Heffernon. E, the genius robot, sees the flying object, notices that it is round, and "extrapolates" (his word for "thinks," not mine) that we're still in phys ed class—he figures we've just moved from the gym to a new location. Yes, E thinks food ball is a game—like dodgeball without the basketball court.

So E starts lobbing Tater Tots at Bobby Hatfield.

Tom Heffernon sees E tossing the potato wads and figures the robot is also the guy who nailed *him* with the tangerine. So Tom fires back. He uses his spoon like a catapult and launches a glob of mashed potatoes, which splatters on top of E's head.

Meanwhile, Bobby Hatfield, the kid E nailed with the Tots, sidearms a fistful of lima beans at E.

Robots always sense, think, and act. So first E senses that he is wearing potato glop on top of his head and has lima beans splattered all down his front. Next, he does some quick computations. And finally, in reaction mode, he fires back by scooping up the fruit cup and burger off my tray—and flinging one at Heffernon, the other at Hatfield.

Pretty soon everybody in the cafeteria joins in.

Before long, the food is really flying. Chicken nuggets. Baked beans. Zucchini sticks. It's a mess.

But E saves the best (or worst) for last.

When we're studying science. Back in Mrs. Kunkel's classroom.

CHAPTER
9

You'd think E, a creature of science, would show the subject the respect it deserves.

You'd be wrong.

E disagrees with everything Mrs. Kunkel and the science book are trying to teach us.

"Arthropods are small animals with jointed feet and other appendages attached to their bodies," says Mrs. Kunkel.

"Does that make me an arthropod?" asks E, manipulating his hands and legs. Talk about double-jointed. E can rotate his left foot behind his right thigh—then spin the whole leg around like a corkscrew till the front of his foot is where the heel should be.

So Mrs. Kunkel decides to move off arthropods and teach us about static electricity.

"Let's run a little experiment with a plastic comb and a small fluorescent lightbulb."

"I can spell *fluorescent*," says E.

"Thank you, E. But this is science, not spelling. Now then, static electricity—"

"Correction," says E. "Electricity is never static or motionless, because electrons are constantly circling the nucleus of an atom, which, by the way, is composed of protons and neutrons...."

And BLAH, BLAH, BLAH.

Mrs. Kunkel keeps trying to squeeze a word in edgewise, but the blabber-bot won't let her. He keeps rattling off factoids.

Worse, Error will not, *cannot* shut up. In fact, he starts yammering faster and faster, as if someone has a thumb on his fast-forward button. His already high-pitched voice speeds up and starts sounding like he's been sucking helium out of birthday balloons.

"Static electricity is an imbalance of electric charges within or on the surface of a material."

His silicon-chip brain is so hyperactive it starts generating more static electricity than all the plastic combs in the personal grooming aisle at Walmart.

"The charge remains in place until it is able to move away by means of an electrical discharge, such as this one about to discharge inside my head."

*ZAP! ZIZZ! ZLITZ!*

Sparks spew out of E's ears.

"Shall I spell *Kyrgyzstan* for you now?"

*BZZZNNT! FLOOF! SIZZLEFITZ!*

Smoke pours out of his eyes, ears, and armpits.

You may have already guessed what happens next.

Yep. One of those sparks lands in the paper-recycling bin.

There are bells and sirens, and then the fire department shows up with all sorts of hoses and axes and these really long, pointy poles. One firefighter tosses

a bucket of sand on E's head. Another blasts him in the face with a foaming fire extinguisher.

You guys already know where we go after that: the first-ever parent-teacher-student-robot conference in Mrs. Reyes's office.

The conclusion of E's first day at Creekside? A happy ending—for me, anyway. Because the grown-ups come to what they call a "mutual decision."

E isn't "quite ready" for school yet.

Ha! I could've told them that first thing this morning.

# CHAPTER 10

All righty, so here we are on our way home. I'm the one looking pretty happy.
Mom and Dad? Not so much.

As we pull out of the school driveway, Dad says to Mom, "Don't worry, Liz. You'll figure it out."

Mom mumbles something nobody can understand because she is already in The Zone. Whenever she stares off into space like that, I know her high-powered brain is hard at work, running off to infinity and beyond, noodling out a list of possible solutions to whatever's wrong with E.

She should ask me. I could tell her E's number one problem: School is for kids, not robots.

*Me*, not him.

Robots should stay home and vacuum the floor, make breakfast, or answer the phone. If you want to see how they do outside the house, take them to an automobile factory and let them weld bumpers onto cars or play with the crash-test dummies. But whatever you do, *keep the robots away from me and my school.*

E's LED eyes don't look as bright as they did this morning. His head is a little fried around the edges from where his circuit boards overloaded. And there's still some fire extinguisher foam where his nose would be if he had one.

E's shoulders are sagging and he's making a weird *GLIT! GLORT! BLEEBLE!* sound.

If I didn't know better, I'd say Error was feeling sad.

Well, I'm not going to let it get to me. I cross my arms over my chest and slump back in my seat.

"Look, dude," I whisper to E. "If you ever want to fit in with kids my age, you need to lighten up. Chill."

There's a soft *SUT! FLUT! FLIT!* as E's head pivots left to face me.

"Thank you, Samuel. That is excellent input. I am very adaptive, especially when presented with the proper external stimuli."

"Dude. You're doing it again."

"Pardon?"

"You're, you know, sounding all robot-ish."

"I see. Please excuse my error. I shall strive to do better."

"No worries. We're cool."

"Is that what happens when you chill as you previously suggested?" asks E. "Do you become cool?"

"Yeah. Something like that."

Now E crosses his arms over his chest. "Cool," he says. "Thank you, dude."

When E says that, I actually smile. Just a little.

When we get home, Mom thumbs a remote that looks like a garage door opener. It's the controller for Forkenstein—a headless robotic forklift she uses to haul heavy stuff around in her lab. Forkenstein is all arms and tank treads. Mom opens the door on E's side of the hybrid. Then she toggles the dial on her remote. Forkenstein shoots out his lift arms and grabs hold of E.

"You're going back to the shop for a few minor repairs," Mom says to E with a sigh. "Sorry about that."

"No worries, dude," says E to Mom. "We're cool."

Mom looks a little puzzled. She flips a switch on the bottom of his backpack. The robot's bright blue eyeballs lose all their color. I hear a faint *PLOIP!*

E's head flops forward. Forkenstein hauls E's limp body out of the car. His legs dangle. He sort of looks like he's dead.

Me?

I sort of feel like crud.

As I head inside, I'm also wondering why that SUV is parked at the end of our driveway.

**CHAPTER 11**

All righty, so let me tell you a little about my mom and dad, which maybe I should've done sooner, huh? I guess I really need to organize my stories better. Maybe I should outline before I start writing. That might be good.

Where was I? Oh, right. At home. With a strange car parked at the end of our driveway. But it left as soon as E was tucked away inside Mom's workshop, so I can't tell you any more about that.

So, let's check out my mom and dad.

First, I'll admit they're both mostly nice. Yes, every once in a while, Mom gets a dopey idea like, "Hey, let's make Sammy a bionic brother and send them both to school!" But all in all, she and my dad are thoughtful and extremely intelligent people. They're both in Mensa, this special club for geniuses with high IQs. I'm not exactly sure what they do at the Mensa clubhouse. Probably play chess a lot.

Maddie and I are both super lucky that our parental units are so amazingly smart, especially with all they have to deal with at home. More about that later, too. Promise. (Don't worry, it's in my outline. Really.)

But here's the one humongous problem: Mom and Dad, even though they're both, you know, kind of old (we're talking *over thirty*), completely refuse to grow up.

My dad is an award-winning illustrator/cartoonist. Other dads in the neighborhood have jobs in office buildings or factories. Dad? He stays home all day, wears T-shirts and sloppy shorts, draws ninja warrior robots, and has them say stuff like "Bzzzzt!" and "Fwoomp!" when they explode. He's nice but kind of kooky. He once drew a purple-and-green fire-breathing dragon on roller skates that liked to drink chocolate milk shakes through its nose.

My mom, on the other hand, is an absentminded professor of computer science who teaches in the College of Engineering at the University of Notre Dame. Mom always helps organize ND's National Robotics Week events at the Stepan Center. Last year, there was a robot that could tell jokes.

SILICON-BASED COMEDY
WHY DID THE ROBOT CROSS THE ROAD?
IT WAS PROGRAMMED BY THE CHICKEN!
WAIT. DO NOT DEPART. I HAVE 4,999 MORE....
HA!
JOKE-A-TRON 5000
STAR WARS

My favorite part of Robotics Week was the mechatronic Blue-Gold robot football game featuring the Fighting iBots (instead of the Fighting Irish, which is what ND's real football team is called). The players were all the size of desktop printers but could make all the right moves—passing, blocking, catching, punting.

And, of course, after the game, half the team came home with Mom.

One is still here. Blitzen, the middle linebacker. Now when he runs downfield, he also mows the lawn.

If Mom ever makes me take another robot to school, I sort of hope it's Blitzen.

I'd love to see how *he'd* deal with Cooper Elliot!

# CHAPTER 12

Here are some other things you should know about my mom and dad:

They laugh a lot. I mean *all the time*. They're unbelievably silly.

Mom and Dad also hug a lot, too. Like they're still dating.

"Because we still are," says my dad.

(I just roll my eyes whenever he says that, which is constantly.)

Their love of hugging also means tons of hugs for Maddie and me. That's fine. But...

Did Mom really need to program E to hug it out, too? Because that's something else the crazy robot did on his very dumb, very bad first day of school.

Yeah, I forgot to mention it. Actually, I was kind

of trying to block it out of my memory. But seriously, did E have to bear-hug me like that when I came out of the boys' room?

"Did you remember to wash your hands, Samuel?" he asked.

"Uh, yeah."

"I am so proud of you!"

That's when he hugged me. Just wrapped those powerful, multi-jointed arms around me, contracted his hydraulics, and squeezed tightly.

Now, when a robot hugs you, your feet don't stay on the floor very long. You also have a hard time breathing. Plus, everybody within fifty feet of the hugfest busts a gut laughing.

Especially Cooper Elliot. "Aw! Sammy's big bwudda wuvs him!"

Here's something else about my mom and dad: They totally love rock and roll. For fun, both my parents are in a band called Almost Pretty Bad. Because they are.

Pretty bad.

*Almost.* (Sometimes they're closer to Totally Awful.)

Dad plunks out the deep bass notes. Mom is the lead singer. Mrs. Reyes, the principal at Creekside, plays drums.

The most talented member of the group is a robot named Jimi who plays electric guitar and flashes colorful lights in sync with the musical notes he's plucking. I think Mom got the idea for Jimi when she saw a *Guitar Hero* game tossed in the neighbors' trash about a month after Christmas. Jimi, the lead guitar, is actually Pretty Good, and that makes the rest of Almost Pretty Bad sound, well, Even Worse.

**CHAPTER 13**

**O**kay, I need to start a new page for this.

My mom's many robots.

I'm not kidding—they're everywhere in our house, and in our yard, and in the garage, and in Mom's workshop. There's even a robotic toilet paper dispenser in my bathroom that Mom made out of a recycled SaladShooter.

My mother has so many robots in various stages of construction, we had to buy the house next door to ours and turn it into her workshop.

Now, I know what you're thinking: "Wow. Living with all those robots? That must be really, really, really cool."

Well, it really, really, really isn't.

You would not like life in a house of robots. Trust me—I've lived in one my whole life!

Robots—meet 'em and weep.

Scrubmarine is a scum-sucking underwater robot who cleans swimming pools the way snails clean the slimy grime off aquarium glass. (By the way, we don't have a swimming pool. Go figure.)

Mr. Moppenshine cleans our house. His three feet are made out of spongy stuff, towel-y stuff, and

buffer stuff so he can simultaneously mop, dry, and polish the floor wherever he rolls, leaving his hands free to dust, fluff pillows, and create amazing flower arrangements.

McFetch is our robot dog. Drone Malone is a helicopter robot that sometimes does traffic reports for a local radio station. Brittney 13 is a girl robot Mom programmed to experience "adolescent human emotions."

Constantly.

All of the time.

We're talking day and night, people.

You do *not* want to be anywhere near Brittney 13 when the new issue of *Tiger Beat* magazine comes out, especially if One Direction is on the cover.

Four is a robot that performs at the level of a four-year-old human. (Can somebody tell me what the point of *that* is?) He says "Why?" a lot, can count to ten, and enjoys telling people to "shut up." He could also brush his own teeth if, you know, he had any.

There are dozens of other robots, whizzing and whirring around our house and over in Mom's lab—too many to mention here.

Thankfully, none of them have ever claimed to be my brother. E's the only one who ever tried that stunt.

But he's not really claiming (or saying) anything right now.

He's just hanging out in Mom's robot workshop. Literally.

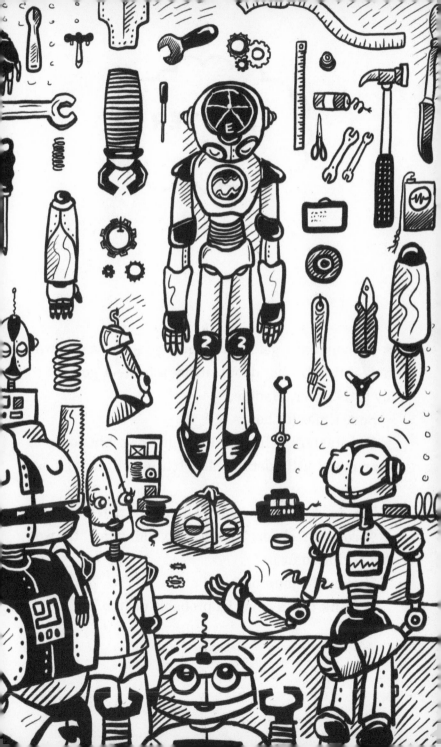

**CHAPTER 14**

**W**henever I get a little nutzoid—the way I was after E's big debut at my school—I go talk to my little sister, Maddie.

Sometimes for hours.

For starters, I fill her in on my day. She loves to hear every little detail. McFetch usually hangs out with us.

The day E got suspended, I had loads to tell Maddie.

"I sort of feel sorry for E," says Maddie. "He was just trying to fit in."

"I guess," I mumble.

"I think that's what I'd probably do, too."

# E's VERY BAD DAY

HOW CAN NUMBERS BE NEGATIVE?
WHAT DID YOU GUYS DO IN ENGLISH?
WHY?
HOW ABOUT SCIENCE?
COULD YOU?
BUT THERE'RE TREES? IN OUTER SPACE?

Okay. Time out. I need to tell you some other stuff about Maddie. But I'm just going to report the facts because Maddie wouldn't want this to sound like a big deal.

"It totally isn't for me" is what she always says whenever this particular subject comes up. "It just is what it is."

But sometimes I can tell it's a much bigger deal for her than she'd ever let on.

See, Maddie suffers from SCID. I wish that stood for *swirl cones in Disney World* or something. It doesn't. SCID is short for *severe combined immunodeficiency*. Basically, it means Maddie has a lot of trouble fighting off any kind of infection. If somebody sneezes in her general direction, Maddie could end up with pneumonia.

So she hardly ever leaves the house. In fact, Maddie hardly ever leaves her own room. That's why our family pet is a germ-free robot dog. Why Mr. Moppenshine is constantly cleaning and disinfecting everything.

Once every three or four weeks, Maddie gets what's called an IVIG—an intravenous immunoglobulin treatment. The IVIG gives Maddie the antibodies to fight off infection that her body can't. A nice nurse named Ms. Ruocco comes to our house with the bags, tubes, and needles.

I don't know if I could stand someone poking my arm like that once a month, but Maddie always says it's "no biggie." Needles are one of my weird phobias, right up there with any kind of heights. But Maddie could probably get a shot on the edge of the Grand Canyon and be totally fine.

By the way, about one in every two hundred thousand kids is born with SCID.

I wonder if they're all as amazing as Maddie.

# CHAPTER 15

I know all this SCID stuff sounds pretty SAD—and it is sometimes—but Maddie refuses to be bummed out about it or anything else.

That's just one of the bazillion reasons why my sister is my number one best friend in the whole world. She's always in a good mood. She even likes her annoying tut-bot, Tootles.

That's what she calls the automaton that Mom designed to homeschool her. The thing (one of Mom's first talking robots) drones on in a dull, monotonous voice. He sounds like he's talking out of his nose. Studying with Tootles is a little like playing *Jeopardy!* with your most boring uncle.

"Studying with Tootles isn't as much fun as going

to a real school would be, I guess," says Maddie. "But I love learning. I sometimes think my brain is the healthiest part of my whole body."

At Maddie's home school, there is no recess. No book fair. No choir or band. No running around in the grass like a crazy person whenever the weather's nice outside.

That makes me feel kind of sad, even if Maddie says, "It's no big whoop," like she always does.

An air-filter machine runs in Maddie's room,

24/7/365. The Breakfastinator is set up in her room, too, because everything about the automatic food dispenser is totally sterile and hypoallergenic.

I can pretty much go in her room anytime I want (after knocking first), but I still have to use hand sanitizer. That's why there are Purell pumps mounted on just about every wall. Did you know that washing your hands is the best way to stop the spread of germs? If you lived at my house, you would.

I don't have to wear a disposable mask when I visit Maddie (unless I'm sick with something), which makes it a whole lot easier to eat breakfast with her. Most visitors have to "mask up" like bandits before they can enter Maddie's room.

Maddie, of course, usually turns the masks into some kind of funny joke because she knows everybody feels weird the second they slip one on.

She always makes sure everybody else feels great—even when she doesn't.

Like I said, my little sister is pretty incredible.

**CHAPTER 16**

**H**ey, the doorbell's ringing!

Actually, it's not a bell—it's another one of Mom's robots, Dingaling the doorman. Dingaling's eyes are motion detectors. The outdoor android automatically rings a bell and shouts like Paul Revere whenever somebody shows up on our front porch.

I'm guessing it's Harry Hunter Hudson, or as I sometimes call him, "Triple H," or just "Trip."

Since he's here, this is probably a good time to tell you about Trip, my *second*-best friend in the whole wide world.

Okay, I'm not trying to be mean or anything, but here's the best way for me to describe Trip: Think of the kid who's the clumsiest klutz, the biggest butterfingers, or the most bumbling fumbler in your whole school.

Now think about the kid who says all the wrong things at all the wrong times, day in and day out. The guy who makes fart jokes. In church.

Now think about the kid who wears goofy clothes, carries a goofy backpack, and walks around in unbelievably goofy socks and shoes.

With me so far?

Okay. Combine all that with the kid who brings PB-and-banana sandwiches to school for lunch *every day*. We're talking Monday through Friday without a break. And make sure you picture those peanut butter

COMPOSURE, SIR!!!

2ND BFF

WOOSH!

sandwiches wrapped in wax paper and bouncing around inside a dented-up Snoopy lunch box.

Now make him extremely annoying.

That's Harry Hunter Hudson, Triple H, Trip. All of the above.

Now, having an annoying and extremely odd best friend—or even a *second*-best friend—like Trip doesn't exactly make me super popular at school.

Fine. I don't care.

Well, I do. A little.

But, hey—I'm loyal to Trip. We are (and always will be) second-best friends forever. That's our deal and we're sticking to it. We've been second-besties basically ever since we were both in diapers, back when Trip was just Harry Hunter Hudson. And, yes, he was annoying even then.

Trip just wouldn't be Trip if he didn't drive everybody (including me) nuts.

**CHAPTER 17**

I guess I'm telling you about Trip so you'll understand why I was so freaked out when Mom made me go to school with E.

See, Trip and I already have something of a reputation for being, well…different.

At least that's what the kids who, for whatever reason, get to decide who's cool and who isn't think about Trip and me. The two of us have permanent seats at the losers' table in the cafeteria.

To prove my point, let me bring you up to speed on the Trip-and-Sammy highlights reel.

For openers, that kid Cooper Elliot, the one who calls me "Dweebiac," has been picking on Trip and me since as long as either one of us can remember.

In fact, back in second grade Cooper Elliot made both of us cry in front of the whole entire school—not to mention everybody's parents and grandparents.

Here's another blast from the past: Remember how I told you that Trip always says the wrong thing at the wrong time? Well, once when we were in third grade, Mrs. Reyes, the principal, finally picked Trip and me to do the morning announcements.

Did you notice how I said "once"?

After I listed the lunch menu (corn dogs, potato spudsters, yogurt, and string cheese), Trip leaned into the microphone and said, "Please join us for a moment of silence and medication."

I think he was supposed to say "meditation," but Mrs. Reyes took Trip's advice and popped a few aspirin the second we were done. I'm pretty sure we gave her a splitting headache.

During lunch, Trip is mocked on a daily basis for his peanut-butter-and-banana sandwiches.

PEANUT BUTTER & BANANAS

IT'S WHAT'S FOR LUNCH!

He also annoys anyone within ten feet of our table because he has this loud, open-mouthed, tongue-smacking way of eating his sandwiches because all that peanut butter kind of glues the bread and banana bits to the roof of his mouth.

Totally unacceptable.

So as you can see, I really don't need my "bro-bot's" help to make me unpopular at school.

Trip and I are doing a fine job all on our own.

# CHAPTER 18

**M**y point is that Trip likes to hang out with Maddie as much as I do. He has to wear a disposable mask when he goes in her room, though. The mask is actually a bonus in Trip's case. It cuts down on his peanut-butter-and-banana breath.

McFetch, the germ-free robo-pooch, is mostly Maddie's dog. He keeps her company while Trip and I are at school during the day. I think Maddie's tutor robot is afraid of McFetch—if it's possible for robots to feel fear. McFetch likes to sniff and snort at Tootles's roller-skate-style feet. Maybe they smell like bacon.

Mr. Moppenshine is also a frequent visitor to Maddie's room. He keeps every surface super sanitized and brings Maddie her dinner every night.

# A DAY IN THE LIFE OF MR. MOPPENSHINE!

He also restocks the sterile serving tubes on the Breakfastinator.

Mr. Moppenshine even organizes everything in the refrigerator by height and tosses out any fruit, vegetables, or yogurt the second they hit their expiration date.

Sure, all of Mr. Moppenshine's cleaning and tidying saves me from having to do those chores myself. But even so, in my humble opinion, he is, by far, the most annoying robot my mom ever created.

Well, before Error showed up, anyway.

# CHAPTER 19

I really am all over the place, aren't I? Shoulda made a better outline.

Okay, let's talk about my dad, Noah Rodriguez. Don't forget, he was big on Mom's screwy idea to build me a robotic brother, so you guys need to understand a little bit more about him to see why he doesn't always make the most, shall we say, "mature" decisions in the world.

My father lives a double life. Yep. You heard it here first. You see, my dad is also Sasha Nee, the world-famous manga artist who created the supercool series *Hot and Sour Ninja Robots*.

Dad's graphic novels are ridiculously awesome and...

*Wait a minute!*

Where's my mom?

Time-out in our story.

Seriously.

WHERE IS MY MOM?

# CHAPTER 20

Okay, I know exactly where my mother is and what she's doing. I just lost track a bit.

And—I'm still being honest here—I don't like it. Not one bit.

She's out in her workshop.

DO NOT DISTURB!

CYBORG X-ING

CAUTION

DO NOT ENTER

BEWARE!

TURN AROUND!

STOP

WATCH OUT FOR ROBOTS

Yep—the door is locked. The shades are all down.

"I know what you're doing in there!" I shout, pounding on the door with both fists.

No answer.

"Mom? That robot is an accident waiting to happen. The next time, Error could burn down the whole school. Maybe he should just stay home and help Mr. Moppenshine scrub toilets."

Finally, the door creaks open.

"Mom, please—what's the point of this experiment,

anyway? What exactly are you trying to prove?"

"I'm sorry, Sammy. I can't tell you."

"Why not?"

"Because it might not work."

"So?"

"If E fails, the consequences will be devastating."

"What? You'll lose your job?"

"No, hon. Something worse. But…if it works…" Her eyes sparkle like she just swallowed a whole string of twinkle lights. "If E can successfully function at your school and move up, advance through the grades—"

"No! Please! I don't want to be a dweebiac in high school *and* college, too!"

"Sammy? You're standing in the way of progress. Change is a good thing. It's also *inevitable*. It's going to happen whether you want it to or not."

Inevitable.

A very good word to describe my future as a total dweebiac.

**CHAPTER 21**

**B**y the way, *inevitable* is just one of my mother's favorite words.

She has a lot. Here's a quick list:

1. **PERSEVERANCE**
2. **DETERMINATION**
3. **SPUNK**
4. **STICK-TO-ITIVENESS**
5. **DEDICATION**
6. **DOGGEDNESS**
7. **TENACITY**
8. **SOPAIPILLA**

Notice how most of her favorite words mean the same thing? Yep. My mother will keep going, working on whatever needs to be fixed, doing whatever needs to be done—no matter what kind of difficulties, obstacles, or discouragement she may face.

No way was she giving up on E.

As for word number eight, *sopaipilla*, she likes to eat those on special occasions or to celebrate robot breakthroughs. Sopaipillas are, basically, Mexican doughnuts. They're chewy and soft, like Krispy Kremes, but soaked with honey. Dad brings them home sometimes, especially if it's someone's birthday.

Standing there outside her workshop, knowing my mother is inside tinkering with E the Annoy-a-tron, I want to scream a few of *my* favorite words:

1. **WHOA!**
2. **STOP!**
3. **KNOCK IT OFF!**
4. **GIMME A BREAK, MOM!**
5. **PUH-LEEZE?**

But I don't.

Because I know she won't listen. She'll keep on repairing E's fried circuits and reprogramming those "one or two or maybe four" minor miscalculations she made the first time around.

Why?

Because my mother has perseverance, determination, doggedness, and dedication—not to mention spunk, stick-to-itiveness, tenacity, and a whole bunch of other words that all mean the same thing: *She won't quit working on a problem until she solves it.*

So I slump back to my bedroom realizing the horrible truth.

One day soon, my mother will make me take E to school again.

It's inevitable.

**CHAPTER 22**

**M**onday comes and I head back to school.

Thankfully, E isn't coming with me. Despite all her stick-to-itiveness, Mom didn't "get 'im done!"

But she is skipping school and letting a substitute teacher handle all her classes at Notre Dame just so she can spend the day (and night) in her workshop tinkering with E. I think a lot of the other robots around our house are nervous. Mom keeps eyeballing them for spare parts.

It seems E has become my mother's number one priority. Well, except for Maddie. It's almost as if, in my mother's mind, the hunk of junk really is a member of our family.

"But what if she fixes it?" says Trip during gym class.

"She will," I say. "There's no if, and, or but about it."

Trip snort-giggles. "You said 'butt'!"

Sometimes I can't believe Trip is actually the same age as me. "Trip?"

"Yeah, Sammy?"

"How come you always sound like you have asthma when you laugh?"

"Because I laugh backward. Eeh-eeh-eeh. See?"

"Hey, Dweebiacs," shouts Cooper Elliot. "You're dead meat."

Yep. We're playing dodgeball today, and Coach Stringer is off giving Andy Reinhertz a fitness test. That means Cooper is free to tease and harass Trip and me all he wants.

Of course Trip and I were the very last ones chosen when the two captains were picking sides. Poor Jacob Brown—Cooper made him take *both* of us.

At my school, we usually play dodgeball on the outdoor basketball court. Six very hard, rubber-coated foam balls are lined up on the center line. We have to stay behind the out-of-bounds line underneath the basket until the ref shouts "Go!"

Since Coach Stringer isn't around, Cooper appoints himself substitute PE teacher and temporary dodgeball referee.

"Go!" he shouts (after he takes a two-step running head start).

This is what they call the "opening rush." We're supposed to race across to the center line, grab three balls, and start pummeling the guys on Cooper's team while dodging the three balls they're hurling at us.

Did I mention that I run pretty slowly?

Or that Trip runs even slower?

We don't even make it to the center line before Cooper Elliot and his teammates bean us both.

I go down hard when Cooper's ball socks me in the gut.

I almost lose my Cap'n Crunch.

With Trip and me out in the first seconds, our team doesn't stand a chance. We lose the game just like we do every time we play dodgeball.

I guess it could've been worse.
I guess E could've been there.
But tonight, things *do* get worse.
Way worse.
Maddie is sick again.

**CHAPTER 23**

This happens, I'd say, three or four times a year. And it's unbelievably scary each and every time.

Tonight, it's a respiratory problem. Maddie is having a lot of trouble breathing. She also has a temperature "spiking at one hundred and five degrees," according to my mom, who abandoned E the instant Dad texted her in her workshop.

We're waiting for the ambulance, and I guess I look as freaked out as I feel, because Maddie just smiles and says, "No biggie, Sam. Don't get your panties in a twist."

She says it very softly because she can't afford to

waste a lot of the oxygen when she's having so much trouble breathing.

I take her hand and try to smile back. "Whatever you say, sis."

"How...school...?"

"Don't talk, okay? Just breathe. I'll tell you everything that happened today."

She inhales a shallow breath. I can tell it hurts her to do it.

I start talking a mile a minute.

"Okay, today during gym we were playing dodgeball. Trip and I were on the same team, of course, and you should've seen Cooper Elliot's face when I nailed him before he even made it to the center line. Yep. I creamed him. *BOOM! POW!* Knocked him on his butt. After class, Coach Stringer—he's the gym teacher—was telling everybody that he had never seen a dodgeball thrown that hard. He even clocked me with a radar gun. Said I had a ninety-mile-per-hour fastball. I told him I wasn't even trying. I side-armed the thing."

"Really?" Maddie asks with a grin.

"No. But one day it'll really happen. You'll see."

"I can't wait."

"Me neither."

Luckily, we don't have to wait very long for the ambulance.

They come here so often, they know how to find our house.

## CHAPTER 24

"**H**ey, Dave. Hey, Dylan."

Yep. Maddie knows most of the paramedics from St. Joe's. Like I said, they come to our house a lot.

The hospital guys won't let me ride in the ambulance with Maddie, which I sort of understand.

But Mom and Dad won't let me go with them, either.

"Guard the fort, Sammy," says Dad.

"B-b-but—"

"Mrs. Stein is on her way," says Mom.

I'd give them both a look—one of my really squinty

ones—if I didn't know they already had enough to deal with.

Mrs. Stein is our neighbor. She comes over sometimes to "babysit" me even though I haven't been a baby for, like, eight or nine years.

"It's just a term," my mother says whenever I remind her that I'm not an infant.

Anyway, Mrs. Stein is okay. I mean, I like her. Plus, having her babysit me is way better than dealing with Nanny Nano, this rattle-trap child-care contraption Mom invented back when I was maybe three. Nanny Nano thought everything I did was dangerous. She made me cut my hot dogs with a plastic spoon and go to bed wearing a bicycle helmet.

But come on—I'm way too old for any kind of baby-sitter. Human or robotic.

Besides, I want to be at St. Joseph's hospital with my sister, Maddie.

Of course nobody cares what I want.

Not tonight.

Not ever.

CHAPTER
25

One of my mom's favorite lectures—and there are a ton of 'em, trust me—is all about how kids (that means ME!) can't possibly understand all the decisions that adults have to make "for the good of their children!"

EVERYTHING WE DO, WE DO FOR YOU.

EAT YOUR VEGETABLES.

ALWAYS WEAR CLEAN UNDERWEAR.

GOD GAVE YOU A BRAIN— USE IT.

IF YOU GO OUTSIDE WITH WET HAIR, YOUR FACE WILL FREEZE!

$E = Mc^2$

I'M NOT ASKING, I'M TELLING.

UM, ISN'T THAT LECTURE FOR SCHOOL?

"Everything we do, every decision we make, we do for you and Maddie."

That means we have to trust our moms and dads to know and do what's best for us.

Even if, for instance, they tell you to take a robot to school or stay home from the hospital when your sister is really sick and you really want to be there with her.

We can't ask questions—at least, not more than a couple.

Three is the absolute limit. Once I tried to go for four and got shot down, *big-time*.

Tonight, of course, I only got to ask one: "Can I go with you guys?"

You already know the answer.

"No!"

That's why I'm sitting here at home. Totally scared about Maddie and her fever and how hard it was for her to breathe and whatever's going to happen next!

Of course, I'm not totally alone.

Yep. That black SUV is back. Parked at the end of our driveway.

I decide to go find out what the heck they want and how come they're always parking in front of our house.

But two seconds after I start down the porch steps, the SUV drives away.

CHAPTER
26

Okay. Phew. I can start breathing again.

Maddie came home from St. Joseph's Regional Medical Center a couple hours after they rushed her away in that ambulance.

When Mom and Dad helped her up the front steps, she grinned at me—and, like I said, Maddie has *the* best smile of all time.

"It was nothing," she says when she's tucked in her bed again. "False alarm. Total waste of gas *and* sirens. Try not to worry so much, Sammy."

Yep. That's how she deals.

Nothing's ever a "big deal" or a crisis.

I wish I could be more like my little sister and not worry about stuff so much.

I'd give just about anything—including both my autographed Notre Dame football cards (I have Joe Montana *and* Joe Theismann)—to be more like Maddie.

Seriously.

I would.

# CHAPTER 27

Later, when Maddie is sound asleep, I go outside to check out the stars and think about Maddie's advice.

I hear crying.

At first I think it might be Brittney 13. You know—the rolling emoticon. I figure the hysterical, hyperventilating, teenage-mood-swinging robot just picked up some bad news about her favorite boy band—like maybe one of the guys has a new girlfriend.

Then I realize the sobbing sounds are coming from inside Mom's workshop. And the sobs sound like they might be coming from my mom, who hardly ever

cries (except when one of the heavier robots rolls over her toes).

For once, her workshop isn't closed up tighter than spandex on a sumo wrestler. In fact, the door isn't even locked.

I push it open and step inside.

It's kind of dark and shadowy, but my eyes adjust. At a stainless-steel table, sparks sizzle around a shiny mechanical hand attached to an arm that bends like a gooseneck lamp. It's *zizzing* a jumble of colored wires, connectors, and capacitors on a green control board with its fingertips, which are actually soldering irons.

I notice that E isn't hanging on the wall anymore. He's sitting on the edge of the steel table, looking all shiny and spiffy.

If you ever saw my mom's robot workshop, you'd probably think it's amazingly awesome. It reminds me of Santa's workshop at the North Pole, which—spoiler alert—doesn't actually exist.

Santa has more of a factory. In Finland. Where elf-operated robots make all the toys.

So, yeah—the first time you see it, Mom's workshop will knock your socks off.

Personally, I don't like it all that much anymore. To me, it's just a junk-filled place where my mom spends way too much time.

Working.

With the door locked.

**CHAPTER 28**

**T**onight, Mom isn't working.

She's too busy crying.

Mom and I have a pretty nice talk. A real heart-to-heart. And—shocker—it's not about me for a change. We talk about Maddie and how much we love her and how hard it is sometimes to deal with her getting sick—and our getting sick with worry over it.

"But," Mom says with a sigh, "what we go through is nothing compared to what Maddie has to deal with, day in and day out."

I nod even though, as you've seen, Maddie always acts like her situation is no big whoop.

My mom dries her eyes with some kind of screen-cleaning cloth she finds on her workbench.

"Mom? Do you think it'll ever get any easier?"

"I don't know, Sammy. I hope so."

"Maybe one day you and some graduate students at Notre Dame will invent a super-smart, artificially intelligent robot that uses its computer brain to figure out a cure for Maddie and all the other kids with SCID."

"Maybe," she says with a smile.

"Seriously, Mom. It'd be awesome."

She looks at me in a way I don't think she's ever looked at me before. "You're pretty awesome yourself, Sammy Hayes-Rodriguez."

And then neither of us says anything for a while.

We just sit and listen to the robots buzzing and humming all around us.

**CHAPTER 29**

All right, time to lighten the mood! We need a break—for you *and* for me. Even for Trip.

So over the weekend, we go to a Notre Dame college football game.

"Trip can have my ticket," Mom says, even though she's probably the biggest ND fan in the whole family. "I should stick close to home today."

I figure she wants to be with Maddie—just in case there's a Saturday-afternoon emergency. It's only been a couple days since Maddie's fever sent everybody (except me) racing off to the hospital.

So Dad, Trip, and I head over to the campus. A Notre Dame football game at Notre Dame Stadium is the most amazing live sporting event in the entire universe. Seriously. It's better than soccer on Saturn.

A lot of Fighting Irish fans stake out their favorite tailgating spots in the parking lots around dawn.

I text Maddie:

**We didn't pack a barbecue grill or anything, so we're heading over to the Huddle Mart in LaFortune for Quarter Dogs.**

She texts back:

**Smart move.**

Yep. When we go to an ND football game, I keep in constant contact with Maddie back home. Even if she can listen on the radio or watch it on TV, I still like to give her the play-by-play *and* the color commentary. I'm like her eyes and ears on the ground. And that way, it's more like we're there together.

My dad, like my mom, is a Domer. That's what they call anyone who is—or ever was—a student at Notre Dame, on account of the university's most famous landmark: a golden dome at the center of the campus.

On our way to our seats, I text Maddie to let her know Touchdown Jesus is happy to see us. That's what everybody calls this huge mosaic mural on the side of Hesburgh Library that kind of looms over the football stadium.

Normally, my fear of heights would mean that stadium seating is a big, scary deal for me. But because we go so often, and the crowd is so exciting, I barely even notice how high up we are. It really helps that Dad always makes sure we never actually go *that* high.

Since Maddie is also a huge football fan, I text her every time Notre Dame does something good (or even halfway decent) during the game.

The Fighting Irish beat Navy, which is great. Well, for us, not so much for the Midshipmen, which is what the Navy players are called.

What a day. I wish every Saturday in the fall could be a Notre Dame football Saturday.

And more than anything, I wish Maddie could've come to the game with us.

That would've made it the best day *ever*!

Too bad that when we come home, my great day is totally ruined.

Because I find out the *real* reason Mom skipped the ND game.

# CHAPTER 30

O h no, oh no, oh no, oh no!
  While we were at the game, Mom finished
fixing Error!

"Hello, Samuel. I trust you enjoyed today's grid-iron clash?"

Yep. He's *baaaaaack*!

"It was a football game," I tell E. "Not a 'gridiron clash'! A *football game*!"

"I stand corrected."

"Well, at least you're standing," cracks Trip lamely, who, I guess, plans on hanging around and eating dinner with us, too.

"You are correct, Harry Hunter Hudson. I am fully vertical, plumb, and perpendicular."

"Please. Call me Trip."

"Very well, Trip. And might I state for the record that *gridiron clash*, as well as *a pigskin match*, is considered an acceptable synonym for *football game*?"

"That's it," I say, practically exploding. "Where's Mom?"

"Inside," reports E. "Checking up on Maddie."

"Why did she do this to me?" I mumble.

"Actually, Samuel, from my preliminary scans of your internal organs, it does not appear that our mother has done anything to you. Were you in need of repair as well? If so, I am certain she will—"

"No! I don't need any kind of repairs. And she's not *our* mother! She's just *my* mother, okay?"

E raises an eyebrow. Yep. Mom gave him fake eyebrows while he was in her shop.

"What about Maddie?" the robot chirps.

"What?"

"Isn't your mother also Maddie's mother? Isn't that how Maddie became your sister?"

"He has a point," says Trip.

"Fine," I say. "She's Maddie's mom, too. But not yours."

"I didn't say she was," says Trip.

"I'm not talking to you, Trip. I'm talking to Rust Bucket here."

E's knee and hip hydraulics make *ZHURR-CLICK-ZHURR* sounds as he takes one step forward. "Of course she is my mother. Perhaps not in the limited way you look at the world, Samuel. But most certainly Professor Elizabeth Hayes, PhD, is my creator and, therefore, my mother."

Here we go again.

I think E has that particular bit of blabber on some kind of digital loop in his voice box. Either that or Mom gave him a one-track mind.

"I need to talk to Mom," I say to Trip. "She has to tell me where she hid E's off switch. And no way is she making me take this….this…THING to school again!"

I hear a *ZHURR-ZHURR-WHIRR*.

E's staring at me with big, blue, LED eyes.

"Yo, Samuel," he says. "I believe you need to chill, dude."

"Whoa," says Trip. "Did E just say 'yo,' 'chill,' and 'dude'? All in the same sentence?"

"Indeed I did, Trip. I can be very colloquial. It's no biggie. E out."

Yep.

I definitely need to talk to Mom.

**CHAPTER 31**

Remember that thing I said about three being the absolute limit on questions you can ask your parents?

Well, once again, I'm shut down after only ONE!

"How come you fixed Error?" I ask my mom.

She and my dad are in the kitchen, where Mr. Moppenshine is making dinner.

"Samuel?" Mom says in her firm but calm voice—the one that lets everybody, including a lecture hall filled with rowdy freshmen, know who's in charge. "E's proper name is Egghead, not Error."

"Or his name could be Einstein Jr.," says Dad. "But I like Egghead."

I ask my question again. Yep. The same one—but

with different words: "How come you fixed the stupid thing?"

Oops. Mom does *not* like those words.

"E is not stupid," she says. "In fact, E has one of the most highly advanced artificial intelligences I've ever engineered."

"I know," I mumble. "I heard him spell *Kyrgyzstan*. Over and over and—"

Now Mom is glaring at me. Mr. Moppenshine, too.

"Samuel?" she says again.

Mr. Moppenshine just makes *tsk, tsk, tsk* noises and shakes his head.

"Yes?" I kind of gulp it.

"I've already told you how important this experiment is."

"But you won't tell me *why*!"

"Because it may fail. Besides, you don't really need to know *why* I made E. Not yet, anyway. You just need to take him to school with you on Monday."

"I agree with your mother," says Dad. "One hundred percent. This is a very important experiment. We all need to do everything we can to make sure it's super successful."

"But I don't want to!"

Yes. I sort of sound like a kindergartner who doesn't want to take a nap on his blankie because he's having too much fun playing with blocks.

"Frankly, Samuel," says my mom, "I really don't care what you do or do not want to do."

"But, Mom," I whine, "what about all that junk you said about parents doing what is best for their children?"

"This *is* what's best, Sammy."

"Um, no, it is not. Not for me. If I go to school with E again, Cooper Elliot and that bunch will murder me. E will cause another disaster."

"No. He will not. I have addressed all of E's safety issues."

"Really? What about the bit where he calls me his brother and all the other kids laugh and call me Robo-bro and the Dweebatronic? What about *my* safety?"

Mom sighs again. "Fine. Have it your way, Samuel. You don't have to help. E can go to school by himself."

"Fine back at you," I say. "By the way, I'm not taking the bus to school on Monday morning. I'm riding my bike."

"Fine," says Mom. "So will E."

*Really?* I think. *The robot can ride a bike?*

Impossible.

# CHAPTER 32

**M**onday morning comes and nothing seems impossible anymore.

E can ride a bike! And to make things worse, his bike is way cooler than mine.

I'm so angry I scoop up the basketball I left lying in the driveway last night and, using both hands, fling it at the garage door. Hard.

Very hard.

The garage door rattles. The ball ricochets and sails into the lawn behind Mom's workshop, where it bonks Blitzen, who's mowing the grass, in his boxy butt.

"Way to handle the ball, bro," says E, perfectly balanced on his high-tech BMX bike even though it's not moving.

Yep. He can balance like a unicyclist but without

pumping the pedals back and forth. The robot has very good gyroscopes.

"Perhaps," E continues, "in a few years' time, you will hurl a Hail Mary pass in the final seconds of a game to secure victory for the Fighting Irish of Notre Dame in what will become celebrated as a gridiron classic."

"It's called football, Egghead. Foot. Ball."

"True. But because of the parallel lines marking yardage, the football field resembles a griddle, or grid-iron, on which to broil meat or—"

I've heard enough. Like, hours ago. So I tell E to stick a sock in it.

"I do not wear socks," he replies. "Besides, I don't know where you would have me stick this stocking."

"In your piehole."

"As I also do not ingest pie, I do not believe I am equipped with such an opening."

"Never mind."

I hop on my bike.

E pumps his pedals.

We're off.

I can't lose the stupid biker-bot. So I pedal harder,

hoping E is only programmed for one speed—slow.

But I hear a *ZHURR-CLICK-ZHURR* or two and E is right beside me, matching my pace.

Will the horrors upon horrors ever cease? Probably not.

CHAPTER
33

I take a sharp left on Bertrand Street.

E mirrors my move.

"Samuel? Might I suggest we take the next legal right turn and proceed north to Roger Street? According to my internal GPS, that route would be much more efficient."

"No!" I holler. "My bus takes Roger Street. I don't want anybody to see me riding to school with *you*."

"But we are not riding with each other. For that to be possible, Mother would need to construct a bicycle built for two, also known as a dual-drive tandem."

"She's not your mother!" I yell, and take a hard left.

Yep. I'm heading *away* from the school, hoping E's internal compass will force him to keep heading north and west to Creekside.

But it doesn't.

He's still following me.

And, of course, we practically run into a bright yellow school bus picking up a whole bunch of kids.

Mr. Hessler, the bus driver, sees me and E.

"Dude!" he cries out. "A bot on a bike! Totally amazing, man!"

Now everybody on the whole entire bus can see us.

Heads bounce up and down in the windows. Fingers point. Girls gasp. Guys applaud.

E responds to his adoring audience by popping off a bunny hop and doing an off-the-chain BMX bike stunt: He totally nails a double tail whip!

The whole bus is cheering.

Me? The only stunt I pull is not falling off my bike when I see how amazing the new and improved E can be.

CHAPTER
34

We go ahead and follow the bus to school.

Everyone is crammed in the back so they can gawk at us through the rear windows and emergency exit.

I glance over my shoulder, and guess what I see?

Yep. That black SUV. It kind of looks like it's following E and me while we follow the school bus.

Fortunately, when we pull in to the Creekside driveway, the SUV keeps on heading up the road.

Unfortunately, a whole mob of kids streams off the school bus and swamps us at the bike rack.

"That was so cool!" says this cute girl Jenny Myers. She's a redhead in Mrs. Kunkel's class—the one I'm in, too (even though Jenny Myers probably doesn't know it).

"How'd you learn to ride a bike like that?" she asks E.

"Easy. By studying video footage of the BMX World Championships."

"You are, like, so totally epic!"

Of course, Jenny Myers is saying all of this to E, not me, the way she would be if this were one of my dreams.

"Big deal," sneers Cooper Elliot as he struts out to see what all the fuss is about. "So the stupid hunk of junk can ride a bike. I've been doing that for years."

I think Cooper isn't used to somebody (or something) else being the center of attention. "What else can you do, Tin Can Man?"

"All sorts of stuff," says Trip, who was on the bus with everybody else. "Right, Sammy? Because Sammy taught his bro-bot all sorts of incredible tricks while Egghead was in the shop. Remember, Sammy? Remember all those tricks you taught E?"

Trip. My second-best friend forever. Still saying exactly the wrong thing at exactly the wrong time.

"W-w-well," I stammer. "I'm not exactly sure—"

Cooper cuts me off. "*You* taught him? That means when this cheap scrap heap isn't on his custom-built bike, your 'brother' the robot is an uncoordinated klutz just like you. Right, Dweebiac?"

I'm about to answer when I hear E whirr forward.

"Actually, Cooper Bernard Elliot..."

"Whoa! How'd you know my middle name?"

"It is listed on your birth certificate in the St. Joseph County vital records online database."

"*Bernard?*" Jenny Myers giggles.

I might actually start smiling soon.

"Trip is correct, dude," E continues. "I do know more tricks. Stand back, please. I am about to bust a move."

With that, E hops into an amazing handstand and walks on his palms all the way up the curving sidewalk to the school's front doors.

Trip and I follow after E. So do all the other kids, except Cooper Elliot, who never likes being in a parade that isn't all about him.

"Good morning, E," says Principal Reyes, who's on front-door duty. "Great to have you back at Creekside."

"Great to be back, Mrs. Reyes," says E, who is still upside down and using his hands for feet. "But I would be remiss if I did not advise you to tie your shoelace as soon as it proves convenient for you to do so."

"Thanks, E. Will do. Okay. Move along, boys and girls and, uh, bots. You have a lot to learn today. And I need to tie my shoe."

## CHAPTER 35

**W**hen we're inside, E flips out of his handstand, does a double somersault in midair, and nails an Olympic-gymnast-style landing. Trip applauds.

"Hey, E—you want half a peanut-butter-and-banana sandwich at lunch today?"

"No, thank you, Trip. I eat electricity, not food. But might I suggest you bring your sandwich to the lunchroom in a plain paper bag today?"

"What? You don't like my Snoopy lunch box?"

"Oh, I enjoy it immensely. However, I also know it is currently worth ninety-five dollars on eBay."

"No way."

"Way. A valuable treasure such as that should be kept in a safe place at all times. Perhaps you should leave it locked up at home in the future?"

"Cool! Thanks for the tip. See you in class, guys."

While Trip hurries off, I turn to E. "How'd you know people make fun of Trip's Snoopy lunch box?"

"I knew no such thing, Samuel. However, I assumed they might."

"What about that handstand? How'd you learn how to do that?"

"Easy. One day, I saw you execute a similar move

for Maddie. If I remember correctly, she smiled."

"Yeah. She usually smiles when I do something extremely stupid like that." Because when I tried to flip out of the handstand, I crashed and burned.

"You are a good brother, Samuel. And please—do not worry, brood, or fret. I will keep my distance from you during normal school hours as you have previously requested."

With a *ZHURR-CLICK-ZHURR*, E lumbers and lurches down the hallway.

The first bell is about to ring, but everybody wants to hang in the hall so they can slap E a high five or shake his hand or ask him what other amazing things he can do.

Me?

I kind of don't exist.

# E AND HIS ADORING FANS!

# CHAPTER 36

Okay, I have to admit it—Mom did an amazing job fixing E.

During language arts, he doesn't start spouting annoying factoids at Mrs. Kunkel about conjunctions or interjections. Actually, he doesn't interject once!

But later in the morning I sure do.

We're working on an art project called the Statue of Me. First, we discuss why the Statue of Liberty is important to America and what it stands for. Then we're supposed to draw our own statues and show what's important to us. Everybody does it with pencils, markers, and watercolors.

Well, everybody except E. He uses clay.

"Wow!" I exclaim when I see his creation.

When it's time for spelling drills, E sits out.

"I have an unfair advantage over my classmates," he explains to Mrs. Kunkel. "I have memorized several different dictionaries. English, Spanish, Mandarin, Farsi, and so forth."

But he does help out anybody who is struggling.

Like Davy Morkal, who can't remember how to spell *believe*.

"If I may offer a bit of advice, Davy," E says, after Mrs. Kunkel says it's okay for him to coach spellers from the sidelines, "never believe a *lie*."

I'm guessing Davy Morkal will never forget that *believe* is spelled with an *l-i-e*.

When I stumble on my word, *misspell*, E tosses me a great hint.

"Remember, Samuel—Miss Pell never misspells!"

Then, during math, E surprises us all.

Mrs. Kunkel gives him a word problem:

"All right, E. Ronnie is in the orchestra. Jonelle is in the band. There are thirty-nine students in the orchestra and twice that number in the band. There are twenty-three boys and thirteen girls in the choir.

WOULD YOU LIKE ME TO CONVERT A FEW IMPROPER FRACTIONS INTO MIHED NUMBERS? COUNT AND COMPARE SIDES, EDGES, FACES, AND VERTICES? BREW A CUP OF COFFEE?

If each student only participates in one group, how many students total are there in the orchestra, the band, and the choir?"

E cocks one of his new eyebrows and says, "Way too many, Mrs. Kunkel."

Yep. E cracked a joke. Everybody laughs, including Mrs. Kunkel.

"Is that your final answer?" she asks him.

"No. However, as I have learned from my bro—er, *friend*—Samuel, sometimes it is wise to interject a little humor into one's daily routine. All work and no play makes E a dull robot. But, jest concluded, let me state that the correct answer to your original question is one hundred and fifty-three students."

"Well done, E. You've earned another gold star."

When it's 11:30, Mrs. Kunkel announces, "All right, everybody, put away your books. It's time for lunch."

*Lunch.*

The last time E tried that, food went flying.

Forget math and spelling.

This will probably be his biggest test of the day.

# CHAPTER 37

When we hit the cafeteria, E doesn't sit with Trip and me at the losers' table.

"As requested," he states, "I will also keep my distance from you during lunch period."

Mom's robot goes off and finds a table all by himself in the farthest corner of the room.

Trip sniffs his armpits. Cups a hand over his mouth and exhales like he's fogging up a car window so he can check out his breath. Yep. Trip does this kind of gross stuff. In public. A lot.

"Why won't E sit with us?" he asks. "Do we smell bad?"

"I don't think E smells, Trip."

"Sure he does. Like a new car."

Yes, Trip is being annoying again.

"What I meant," I explain, "is I don't think Mom outfitted E with, you know, a nose. A robot doesn't need to sniff stuff unless it's McFetch, Maddie's dog. And that's just so he seems more doggish."

Trip unwraps his peanut-butter-and-banana sandwich. By the way, he took E's advice. He didn't bring his Snoopy lunch box to the cafeteria today, and so far nobody's making fun of him.

Meanwhile, E is just sitting over there, all alone, having a cheeseburger, Coke, and fries. Just kidding—he actually has his hands neatly folded on top of the table. I think he might be in sleep mode. Maybe he plugged himself into a nearby wall outlet to recharge his batteries.

Before long, kids who are having today's hot lunch (chicken patty on a bun) start streaming over to E's table carrying their trays.

Anyway, I can't hear what E is saying, but I can definitely hear all the kids crowded around him laughing and giggling and having a great time. Including Jenny Myers. Her giggles are the best.

So, major breakthrough time for Mom's big, super-important experiment. E is playing well with others. Plus, he doesn't hurl any food today.

But he does do some nifty juggling with a banana, two apples, an orange, and a clump of broccoli while telling everybody how important it is to eat five fruits or vegetables every day.

"Guess E doesn't need us anymore, huh?" says Trip. "Guess he's one of the cool kids now."

"Fine," I say. "We don't need him, either."

"I guess not," says Trip. "But you know what?"

"What?"

"I kind of miss him."

"Eat your sandwich."

"Nah," says Trip, pushing it away. "I'm not hungry."

"Yeah. Me neither."

**CHAPTER 38**

Later in the afternoon, during PE class, I can see LE entertaining another gaggle of girls over on the far side of the basketball court.

Mom must've loaded his memory chips with a *ton* of videos from the Summer Olympics.

While E's doing his routine, Trip and I are basically doing our best to hide—hoping nobody ever picks us for today's dodgeball game.

Unfortunately, Coach Stringer will, sooner or later, see our names in his roll book. So that means we're both going to get clobbered. Again.

"Sammy Hayes-Rodriguez?" calls Coach Stringer. "Harry Hunter Hudson?"

"Yes, sir?" We both limply raise our hands.

"You two are on Jackson Rehder's team."

Jackson groans. Cooper Elliot smirks.

Here we go again.

Coach Stringer lines up the six balls at the center of the basketball court.

I feel someone tap me on the shoulder. It's E. "This morning," E says. "In the driveway. Remember how you threw that basketball at the garage door?"

"Yeah."

"Do it again. Simply pretend the dodgeball is the basketball, your opponents are the garage door, and you are livid about having to take me back to school with you."

"Okay. Maybe. Quick question. What's 'livid'?"

"Enraged. Furiously angry. Boiling mad. Fussing and fuming. Hot under the—"

"Okay, okay. I got it."

"Put all your anger into your throw, Samuel. See the ball. Be the ball."

Yep. C-3PO has turned into Obi-Wan Kenobi.

Coach Stringer blows his whistle. "Go!"

I tear across the field.

As I run, I think about what E just said. How I chucked that basketball this morning. How E said I could toss touchdowns for Notre Dame someday.

I reach the center line before anybody else. Maybe I'm not as slow as I thought—especially when I'm "livid." I snatch up one of the balls.

I see Cooper Elliot. He looks as wide as a garage door.

So I hurl the ball at him.

Cooper twists sideways, trying to dodge it.

But my ball is flying too fast. It's streaking flames like a comet. Well, it should've been doing that.

It nails him. Hard.

I'm so surprised, I just stand there admiring my handiwork.

And somebody else on Cooper's team nails me. In the gut. Again.

I don't care. I got Cooper Elliot out first! It's not quite as dramatic as the story I told Maddie, but I'll take it.

And guess who saw me at my personal dodgeball best?

Jenny Myers.

She's standing over by the fence. Right next to E, who has his big right arm fully extended—pointing at me!

# CHAPTER
# 39

**A**fter school, I bicycle home with E.

Every bus in the parking lot is cheering for us. The crossing guard stops traffic so we can breeze on by. Cars honk their horns for us.

Yep. In just one day, E has become the favorite robot of everybody in South Bend, Indiana.

Well, everybody except maybe Trip.

"How come E didn't coach *me*?" Trip had whined after I creamed Cooper. "Why didn't E tell me to 'see the ball and be the ball'?"

"I dunno," I'd said with a shrug. "Maybe because you're not his brother?"

"But I'm his brother's second-best friend. Right? Or am I suddenly in third place behind your little sister and your battery-powered bro-bot?"

I probably should've answered Trip or made him feel better. But I was feeling too good to worry about Trip feeling bad. And, well, Jenny Myers came over to talk to me.

"Egghead told me you've been practicing," Jenny said.

"He did?" I tried my best not to let my whole head, including my ears, turn bright red.

"Uh-huh. At lunch. He said you were getting so good at throwing stuff, you'd probably play quarterback for Notre Dame someday."

How awesome is that?

Long story short, maybe having E go to school with me on a regular basis isn't the worst idea Mom ever had. Maybe hanging out with the E-ster will make life a little easier for me. Maybe it will be good for Trip, too. Maybe not today, but soon.

A couple blocks from home, E raises his arm to signal a stop. So I do.

E climbs off his bike. I straddle mine. The robot marches right up to me. Have I mentioned how tall he is?

"Samuel?"

"Yeah?"

"We have to talk."

UH-OH. DID MOM PROGRAM E TO GIVE ME ONE OF HER LECTURES?

**CHAPTER 40**

So E and I have a little heart-to-hard-drive chat.

And I have to admit something else: Mom actually did an unbelievable job making E, well, kind of almost human. He seems to have feelings. Moods. He can be happy one minute, worried the next. I'm wondering if that's what Brittney 13 was all about. Was she Mom's first attempt to give her robots life-like human emotions?

"I know it is not easy for you to be seen at school with me, Samuel," E says sympathetically. "I feel your embarrassment."

"Well," I confess, "I wasn't so embarrassed today. You were awesome in class. And at lunch. And especially during gym class. You're totally different than you used to be."

"I have grown and adapted, Sammy. I have also learned from you."

"Me? No way."

"Way."

"But you're super intelligent."

"And you, Sammy, are wise in the ways of the world."

"I am?"

"Definitely. I am not certain I could navigate my way through Creekside without your expert guidance."

Yep. Mom's robot is kind of kissing my butt. I like it.

"I will help you as well as Harrison Hunter Hudson anytime you two want me to," says E. "Or I'll back off. Your call. Totally up to you."

"Great."

"One more thing, Sammy. And I just want you to think about this. Trust your mother. Elizabeth is very smart, and she loves you very much. The same goes for your father, Noah."

"Um, thanks. But I already know that my dad's first name is Noah. You don't have to ID him every time you talk about him."

"My bad. Like every other sentient being on the

planet, I have certain flaws. I am not perfect, Sammy."

"I know," I say. "For one thing, you use words like *sentient*."

"Sorry. It means conscious, alert, aware."

"So use one of those words. They're easier for people to understand."

"Will do. As previously stated, I am not perfect."

"I know. But guess what, E?"

"What?"

"Not being perfect makes you even better."

**CHAPTER 41**

Okay, this is me being super honest again: I have to admit that school has kept getting better and better since E came back.

All of a sudden my table in the cafeteria is the cool table—filled with all kinds of kids who have never been cool before. Since E doesn't really need to eat during our lunch period, he just sits there and tells us funny stories and jokes. The ones I taught him. Well, I let E borrow my *Big Book of Yuks and Chuckles*, but E keeps telling everybody the jokes are mine.

Our new pals laugh so hard, chocolate milk shoots out their noses.

There's only one slight problem.

Remember that table way off in the corner where E used to sit?

Well, that's where Trip sits now. All by himself. With nothing but his peanut-butter-and-banana sandwiches.

I've asked Trip to sit with me and E. Three times. Once for every one of his names.

All three times, I got the same answer: "No, thank you. Have fun with your new bro-bot, XSBFF."

It took me a little while to crack Trip's code, but I'm pretty sure XSBFF means *Ex-Second-Best Friend Forever*.

# CHAPTER 42

The very next day, Trip comes to school with his very own robot.

I kid you not.

It's only about eighteen inches tall, and it wheels down the hall very, very *slooooooowly*. Trip has both his hands stuffed inside the front pocket of his hoodie. I think that's where he's hiding the remote control for his little plastic friend.

I'm guessing Trip bought the RC robot on eBay. Or maybe they sell toy-bots at Radio Shack. Anyway, it's silver with blinking eyeballs and flashing, multi-colored shoulder lights. Its square head swivels back and forth a lot—for no apparent reason.

It talks, too.

"You are my master now," it says in a tinny voice that comes out of a speaker the size of a dime. "Request instructions!"

"Walk," says Trip.

"I can go for a walk with you," says the robot cheerfully.

Then the gizmo starts flashing all its lights and scooting up the hall while playing organ music and whistling. The tune is "Deck the Halls." Don't ask me why.

Trip pretends like he just saw E and me gawking at him.

"Oh, hello, Samuel. E. Meet RC. He's *my* bro-bot. And he can do all sorts of cool stuff E can't."

"Really?" I say. "Like what?"

"He has weapons!"

"Please, Trip," suggests E, "do not demonstrate your robot's weapons capabilities on school property."

Trip, who, I'm guessing, is still mad at E and me for the whole dodgeball thing, doesn't listen. "Why not? Afraid RC will totally show you up, E?"

"Negative."

"Yeah, right. You're just jealous. Watch this!"

"Request instructions!" chirps the little robot.

"Fire at will!"

"Ready, shoot!" says the robot. Then it makes squiggly *BLOOP-BLOOP-BLOOP* alarm sounds and shoots miniature foam rubber disks out of its mouth.

Later in the day, Trip and his new "first-best friend in the whole galaxy" (his words, not mine) are a huge hit in the cafeteria. Especially when Trip loads the toy-bot's mouth cannon with banana slices peeled off his sandwich instead of those foam rubber disks.

But then a peanut-butter-smeared banana discus flies across the lunchroom and—*SPLAT!*—smacks Cooper Elliot right between the eyes.

Mr. Wymer, who's on cafeteria duty, hauls Trip off to the principal's office.

That's probably a good thing.

Otherwise, Cooper Elliot might've smooshed Trip flatter than one of those banana slices after they hit the wall, the floor, or his face.

CHAPTER
43

E carries all our new lunch buddies' trash-filled trays (he can balance, like, fifteen at a time) to the dirty-tray window.

EMPTY TRAYS HERE

"What are we going to do about Trip?" I ask. "He only did that banana-flinging stunt with his remote-controlled robot because he's mad at us."

"You are most likely correct, Sammy."

"Now Cooper's going to clobber him."

"Don't worry. As I promised, I will defend Trip."

"Great. But how do we stop Trip from doing something even goofier?"

"Perhaps we need to make him feel welcome in our circle of friends. The same way you have now made me feel welcome in yours."

"Um, I didn't really have enough friends for a circle till you came along, E. Just Trip."

"All the more reason for us to actively assure him that he is still your best bud."

"Second-best," I say. "Maddie comes first."

"You, of course, are correct, Sammy," says E. "My bad."

Yep. The robot I used to call Error now admits when he makes one.

"No biggie," I say.

"Cool," says E.

"We need a plan, E."

"Indeed we do, bro."

And then we knock knuckles and do a secret finger wiggle—the way Trip and I used to all the time.

"Um, any idea what that plan should be?" I ask.

"Working on it," says E.

"Yeah. Me too."

# CHAPTER 44

After E and I complete our silent-reading period in the afternoon (E's a very fast data scanner—he finished Charles Dickens's 736-page novel *David Copperfield* in sixty seconds), we're able to work up a quick plan.

"You will need to contact Mother," E whispers.

"Already texted her," I whisper back. "She'll be here five minutes after dismissal. In costume."

"Cool," says E.

"We go directly to the bike rack," I remind him. "No stopping to sign autographs."

E nods. He understands. His fans might be disappointed, but saving Trip's butt comes first.

The final bell rings. E and I get to the bike rack before anybody else.

I figure it might take Trip a little while to exit the building. Don't forget—his brand-new, remote-controlled bro-bot moves slower than most snails when they're crawling through a swamp filled with syrup.

I check the parking lot and look for Mom's van.

I don't see her, but I do see that black SUV again. It's parked in the street right in front of the school building.

"I think that car is following me," I say. "I see it all the time."

E makes some *ZHURR-WHIRR-ZHURR* noises as he rotates his head so he can line up his eyeballs with the SUV. Next I hear a *KWEE-VROON* sound as his ice-blue LEDs telescope out about an inch. Then there's a *CLICKETY-CLUNK-CLUNK* as his eyes retract.

"Not to worry," he reports. "I scanned the SUV's license plate. Indiana Notre Dame vanity plate AA999. Using my internal Wi-Fi, I ran that tag number through both the police and FBI databases. The vehicle in question does not pose an imminent threat."

"You're sure?"

"Positive."

"Then why is that same SUV always popping up in weird places?"

Those new eyebrows Mom gave E? They twitch a little.

"Unknown," he says.

"It's been parked outside our house a bunch of times," I say. "It followed us to school that day you first rode your bike."

"Really?" says E, his voice cracking a little on the vowels. "Fascinating."

And you know what?

I think E's lying to me.

"You're sure that creepy SUV isn't dangerous?" I say.

"Affirmative."

"And we don't have to worry about the creeps driving it?"

"Affirmative."

"E?"

"Standing by."

"You're sounding all robot-ish again."

"I'm sorry. Forgive me. I beg your pardon."

I don't push it because finally Trip comes out the front doors with his toy robot shuffling along beside him. It's doing "Deck the Halls" again.

Trip must've accidentally pushed a button on his hidden remote, because the little robot suddenly chirps, "I can dance with you!" Then it starts playing disco music, pumping its arms, and swiveling from side to side in time to the beat. "Let's dance together!"

That's when Cooper Elliot and maybe six of his thuggy buds shove open the doors and storm out to the sidewalk to surround Trip and his little disco-dancing friend.

But I don't think Cooper and his buddies came out to dance.

CHAPTER
45

"That is the dinkiest, dweebiest robot I've ever seen!" sneers Cooper.

"I-I-I..." Trip's actually trembling.

"You think you can have your remote-controlled bucket of bolts shoot bananas at me and not pay the price?"

Cooper is pounding his fist into his open palm. Trip is still trembling.

"I-I-I..."

It's time for me to spring into action.

"Hey, guys," I say, strutting over to join the clump of bullies around Trip and his miniature bro-bot. (Fortunately, the annoying thing's batteries just died, so it isn't disco dancing anymore.)

"Thanks for taking care of X-14 today," I say to Trip.

"What do you know about this, Dweebiac?" says Cooper.

"Just that X-14 is a top-secret project my mom is working on at Notre Dame in the advanced robotics engineering lab. Something to do with the United States Air Force. Oh, and saving the world from the forces of evil. That's basically X-14's job."

"Get out," says Cooper, knocking over the toy robot with the side of his foot. "That little disco-dancing dweebomatic works for the Air Force?"

"That is correct," says E, who has *ZHUSH-SHICKED* over to join us. "Why, when I was in the lab, we all wished we could be as stealthy and sophisticated as X-14. The military is counting on him."

Cooper blows E a lip fart. "Ha! What for?"

And that's when, right on cue, Mom makes her entrance.

# CHAPTER 46

**M**om's brought along two of her graduate assistants from ND—Wendy Garland and Joshua Chun—to make her entrance even more dramatic.

"Boys, I'm afraid X-14's mission is classified," Mom says in her most serious professor voice. "However, I am at liberty to divulge that one of X-14's many skills is to distract our enemies with diversionary tactics."

"By dancing," adds Wendy Garland.

"*Disco* dancing," says Joshua Chun.

"Behind enemy lines," says Mom. "Thank you, Trip, for putting him through his paces for me today."

"Um...you're welcome?" says Trip.

"Now, if you'll all please step aside," says Mom. "We need to rush X-14 back to the lab."

"We have new orders," whispers Wendy Garland.

"They want him at Grissom Air Force Base, pronto," says Joshua Chun as he packs the toy robot inside a very official-looking briefcase—complete with foam slots to cradle the high-tech cargo.

All the boys who were about to beat up Trip start oohing and aahing.

"I think he's going to Kyrgyzstan," says E. "Shall I spell that for you?"

"No time," says Mom. "And boys? Loose lips sink

ships. Let's keep X-14 and his secret mission *secret*. See you at home, Sammy, E. And, Trip, once again, on behalf of a grateful nation, thank you."

Mom and her grad students salute Trip and then hustle off to our minivan with "X-14."

"Wow," says one of Cooper's buds. "That is so awesome."

"Totally," says another.

Fuming, Cooper Elliot stomps off to his school bus. But all the other guys are patting Trip on the back and slapping him high fives.

"So you train robots for Notre Dame? Are you, like, a spy?"

"I'm sorry," says Trip. "That information is classified."

Then he shoots me and E a wink.

I think we're all second-best buds again.

**CHAPTER 47**

A couple days later, we're called to a special assembly in the gym. Dr. Scientrific—a guy with curly hair, a wild mustache, and a wireless microphone headset—is going to show us how much fun science can be.

Woo-hoo.

We file in by grade and have to sit on the floor behind these miniature orange safety cones, leaving an aisle up the middle. I think that's because the fire department says we have to have a "quick means of egress."

You see, Dr. Scientrific does a lot of stuff with fire shooting out of beakers and balloons that magic-ally inflate when you hook them up to a pop bottle

filled with baking soda and vinegar. It's all kind of advanced (and a little scary) for the younger kids. So this assembly is only for third graders and up.

I'm sitting in the very back row. E is squatting beside me. He can do that without his knees hurting. For hours.

Trip has decided to give Cooper Elliot and the rest of the goons at Creekside some fresh ammo for their insults by sitting down front in the first row. With the third graders.

What can I say? Trip *loves* science.

After doing some pretty neat tricks with clear jars of liquids that turn bright red, white, and blue to teach us about chemical reactions, Dr. Scientrific sees E squatting in the back row. His eyes nearly bug out of his head.

"That's our newest student, E," says Principal Reyes.

"Well, E would be the perfect volunteer for my next demonstration!"

"No, thank you, Doctor Scientrific," says E, very politely. "I prefer to observe rather than participate."

But the whole gym starts chanting, "E! E! E!"

E doesn't have much choice.

E lumbers up the center aisle. Dr. Scientrific twists a valve on the portable Bunsen burner he has on his little magician's table. The nozzle hisses. When the scientist sparks a flint near the gas jet, it immediately turns into a bright blue flame.

"Ooh! Ooh!" I hear Trip kind of shout as he flails his arm around in the air over his head again. "Be super careful! E's shell is made out of plastic! It's extremely flammable! It could melt!"

The nutty professor shoots Trip a look, slips on his safety goggles, and ignores the warning.

Uh-oh.

I have a funny feeling we're about to see the South Bend Fire Department in action again—real soon.

# CHAPTER 48

"So, E, do you have twenty dollars I can borrow?" the visiting scientist says when the two of them are behind the table together.

"Negative," says E, and the whole audience laughs. "I do not carry cash."

"Because he's nothing but a talking trash can!" heckles Cooper Elliot. Before the teachers can figure out who hurled the insult, Cooper ducks down behind a wall of kids.

But from where I'm sitting, I can see that Cooper has a thick rubber band strung between the thumb and index finger of his left hand. His right hand is fidgeting with a paper clip.

One of those big, black binder kinds of clips.

"I have a twenty," says Trip from the front row.

"Great," says Dr. Scientrific. "Come on up."

Dr. Scientrific takes the twenty-dollar bill from Trip. "Rule number one when doing this experiment? Never use your own money!"

More laughs.

"All right, E. It seems I forgot my tongs today. I noticed that your hands are actually clamps."

"That is correct. My articulated digits give me a great deal of manual dexterity."

"All right," says Dr. Scientrific, "grab this twenty-dollar bill. Good. Now dip it into this solution."

"Wait!" says Trip. "What's in the bowl?"

"A mixture of tap water and household rubbing alcohol. Go ahead, E. Soak the money in the solution. Great. Now light the bottom."

E cocks a hydraulic eyebrow. "Are you really a doctor? What you suggest seems dangerous."

"What? Haven't you ever heard of 'money to burn'?"

"Of course. It means 'to have a lot of money and spend large amounts on things that—'"

"Just light it, E," says Dr. Scientrific. "This assembly is only supposed to last an hour."

E does as he is told. Fire shoots up from the twenty-dollar bill. It looks like it is completely engulfed by flames. But the money doesn't burn. When the blaze peters out, the bill isn't even charred.

"So, boys and girls," says Dr. Scientrific, "why is it that the money didn't burn?"

Before he can explain, I hear a *FLICK-WHOOSH* and a *PLINK*.

Cooper Elliot scores a direct hit.

The tablecloth erupts in flame as the rubbing alcohol spreads across it like an oil spill.

E tries to stamp out the blaze with his hands.

Which both catch on fire!

# CHAPTER 49

**E**verybody's screaming, screeching, and panicking. Well, everybody except Cooper Elliot. He's giggling.

This is when Trip springs into action.

Yep. Good ol' Harry Hunter Hudson. And can I just say, I am extremely grateful that my second-best friend since kindergarten is a nerd or a geek or whatever you call a guy who LOVES science.

E is super grateful, too.

Because Trip reaches down and pulls up that balloon Dr. Scientrific inflated by shaking a bottle filled with vinegar and baking soda. He plucks the balloon

off the bottle and aims it at the flames flickering all over E's hands.

Then Trip lets out the gas.

The balloon makes the same noise a whoopee cushion does when you sit on it. In two seconds, the fire is totally extinguished.

"And that," says Trip, "is how you smother a fire using the carbon monoxide created when you combine baking soda and vinegar."

Now the whole gymnasium erupts with a cheer.

For Trip!

Not long after, Cooper Elliot is sent to the principal's office. A couple teachers saw what he did.

I hope he's going to be suspended.

For a long, long time.

**CHAPTER 50**

After school, I ride home with Trip and E. Since Trip didn't bring his bike to school in the morning, he has to sit on E's handlebars. I don't think either of them really minds.

CAN YOU HAVE MORE THAN ONE SECOND-BEST FRIEND?

Speaking of home, everything there is way better, too.

Maddie is doing well. She hasn't been rushed to the hospital in weeks. She also aced her first pop quiz of the home-school year.

"Tootles the tut-bot tried to work in some trick questions," Maddie tells me. "But his left eyeball blinks whenever he tries something sneaky like that."

My little sister is even coming out to watch TV in the family room more often. Sure, she has to wear a mask, but still, this is a major breakthrough.

With E working better, Mom is able to focus on a new robot named Hayseed, who does her gardening for her when she's too busy (which is most of the time).

DANG. IT'S SO DADGUM DRY, THE BIRDS ARE BUILDIN' NESTS OUT OF BARBED WIRE, AND THE CATFISH ARE CARRYIN' CANTEENS!

DANG, I'M AS BUSY AS A ONE-EYED DOG IN A BACON FACTORY!

SHOO-WEE! IT'S HOTTER OUT HERE THAN A STOLEN TAMALE!

Dad's busy, too. He just finished writing and drawing a brand-new manga: *Hot and Sour Ninja Robots in Vegas.*

I liked it. A lot. And, amazingly, my approval seemed to make Dad really, really happy.

"I'm really, really glad you like it, Sammy," he said. "Thanks."

As a joke, I gave Dad some of E's gold stars from school.

Trip liked *Hot and Sour Ninja Robots in Vegas*, too.

Yep. He's hanging out at our house again. Eating Mr. Moppenshine's pizza, playing video games with Maddie and me, asking Mom where we keep our peanut butter and bananas.

We are definitely second-best friends again.

And if I have my way, we will be forever.

# CHAPTER 51

School continues to be pretty cool, especially during those three days that Cooper Elliot was suspended. Some days, E, Trip, and I ride our bikes to school, but if it's raining we take the bus.

"We don't want E to rust" is what Trip tells people on the bus when he drips all over them. They don't even complain, really, because there are all sorts of rumors now about how Trip is really an undercover spy.

Meanwhile, E gives out autographs on a regular basis. "But only before school, at lunch, or during recess," he tells his adoring fans. "We do not want to create a disturbance that would inadvertently disrupt your matriculation."

"That means E wants you guys to keep learning stuff," I explain because I'm more or less E's interpreter when he does Bot Talk. But he's getting better at that, too. He's even memorizing slang dictionaries.

"Far out, Mrs. Kunkel," E says to our teacher one day, first thing in the morning. "What is happening? You are certainly looking groovy today."

Too bad he started with slang from 1969.

The little kids in the building love to grab hold of E's arms and legs, hang on, and ride him up the hall.

I can't blame them. I really like hanging out with E, too. It's almost as if we're starting to become buddies, even though I know that's weird and impossible. But sometimes—like when he sighs or wiggles his eyebrows or bops out a beat with a pair of pencils—I forget that E is a robot, that his brain is just a bunch of circuit boards and wires. I even forget that he doesn't really have a heart. Or feelings.

Then again, maybe he does. Maybe he's like Pinocchio.

See, E started out as a kind of puppet, but somehow, magically he turned into a real boy. Well, that's how it seems when I see him with all those little kids hanging off his arms and legs. They're laughing and squealing so much, pretty soon E starts laughing, too. Just like a human would do.

Make that *most* humans.

I almost forgot that Cooper Elliot still goes to Creekside. I got a little too comfortable while he was suspended, I guess.

And Cooper doesn't like to hear little kids laughing. Not when they're laughing at him. Which is what a lot more have been doing ever since E came to school.

And, of course, Cooper blames me for bringing E to school and getting him suspended on account of that slingshot stunt. So I try to avoid the big blowhard as much as possible when he comes back.

Well, one day I can't.

And it almost gets ugly. Really, really, *really* ugly.

**CHAPTER 52**

**T**rip and I are hanging out on the playground during recess. We're sitting on a pair of swings, just shooting the breeze. There's another Notre Dame game this weekend, and we're thinking about asking Dad to let E go with us.

"That would be so awesome," says Trip, swinging high and then jumping off. "Maybe your mom could build him a special set of shoulder pads and he could play!"

"I think that might be against the NCAA rules. E's not a college student. He goes to school with *us*."

"So? Those Rock'em Sock'em Robots get to box all the time, and I bet neither one of 'em ever made it past the first grade."

"Just like you two babies, playing on the swings."

Guess who just snuck up behind us? Yep. Your enemy and mine, Cooper Elliot.

He shoves me hard. I go higher than I've ever been on a swing. Remember my little heights-related phobia? Well, it's kicking in now, in full force. I feel like I might just vomit.

"What's the matter, Sammy?" Cooper sneers. "Scared of heights?"

"No! You just have to let me down. Right now, please. Really, as soon as possible! For very important reasons!"

"Stop pushing him," shouts Trip.

"Or what, peanut-butter breath?" says Cooper. "You going to spit another banana at me?"

"N-n-no..."

"Ha! You two aren't so brave without your big, strong ro-butt buddy, are you?"

Behind me, I hear Cooper huffing and puffing as he shoves me harder and higher.

I also hear familiar *ZHURR-WHIRR, ZHURR-WHIRR* sounds.

"Well," I say, "now that you mention it—"

"Shut up, Samuel Hayes-Rodriguez. By the way, what kind of name is that? Hayes-Rodriguez. Sounds like a disease."

"You are incorrect, Cooper Elliot," chirps E. "It is what is commonly referred to as a hyphenated, or double, surname, combining both of the family names of a child's parents."

Yep. That's what I was trying to tell Cooper.

While he was busy behind me, E snuck up behind *him*.

**CHAPTER 53**

Cooper stops shoving me.

And gets really, really quiet.

I drag my feet on the ground, slow down, and hop out of the swing.

E? He just stands there. Doesn't say a word.

Behind him, parked at the curb, guess what I see? Yep. The black SUV with the dark-tinted windows and the ND vanity plate AA999. Yes, E told me the creepmobile was nothing to worry about, but still...

My focus goes back to E and Cooper. Because E just propped both hands on his hips. With a *SKLURK, SHIF, SHLIK*, he tilts his head to the proper angle for staring down at Cooper.

"Where the heck did you come from?" the bully sputters.

E does not respond.

"He was operating in stealth mode," says Trip. "I think he learned it from X-14."

"He's kind of like a ninja," I add. "One second he isn't there, the next he is."

"It's almost as if he's invisible even though you can see him," says Trip.

"Funny," says Cooper, even though he's frowning.

He makes an ugly face at E.

Well, uglier than usual.

"Somebody needs to pull your plug, you computerized clodhopper."

"If somebody tries," I say, "he might be in for the *shock* of his life."

Trip laughs. "Oh, snap!"

"Be careful, smart-mouths," Cooper snorts at us. "I'm not done with either of you!"

Then he starts walking away. Backward.

"You won't always have your robot friend to protect you."

E's eyeballs lock on Cooper when he says that.

"Of course they will," says E. "I will always be available to provide protection for my brother, Sammy, and his second-best friend forever, Harry Hunter Hudson. By the way, perhaps I failed to mention it when first we met, but my bright blue eyeballs double as freeze-ray guns."

Cooper Elliot's own eyeballs nearly pop out of his skull. He turns tail and runs back into the school building.

"Do you really have freezer beams in your eyeballs?" Trip asks when Cooper is gone.

"No. It is just something I heard Sammy say, back when we first met. I thought it might be a wise and strategic move to repeat it."

So have I mentioned that I like E a whole lot better than I used to?

Well, I guess I should. Because I definitely do!

**CHAPTER 54**

The second I get home, I tell Mom and Maddie about what happened on the playground with Cooper Elliot.

"E was amazing, Mom. He really is like a big brother!"

"What'd he do?" asks Maddie.

"He stood up for me! Trip, too. Wouldn't let Cooper push us around!" I start to imitate E's sort-of-high-pitched voice. "'I will always be available to provide protection for my brother and his second-best friend forever, Harry Hunter Hudson.'"

"He said all that?"

"Yep. Then he kind of glared at Cooper and made a joke about his eyes really being freeze-ray guns."

Maddie laughed. "E tells jokes?"

"Well, I taught him a few."

"Good for you, Sammy," says Mom. "I was hoping you would help E adjust to school life. His artificial intelligence is engineered to learn and grow."

"Well, he's doing way better, Mom. He's not so stiff. Uses a lot less robot words. Doesn't try to show off by being the smartest kid in the class all the time."

"Because you helped him."

I shrug. "I guess."

Then guess what happens? Yep. My mom kisses me. But don't tell anybody, okay? Nobody actually saw it, except Maddie, and that doesn't really count because she's my sister and Mom is her mother, too. You know what I mean.

"You did a good job with E, Mom," I say. "That bot is totally awesome."

Mom and Maddie exchange these private little smiles they do sometimes.

"You should go tell E how you feel," suggests Maddie.

"An excellent idea," says Mom.

"I dunno," I say. "I think E already knows I don't hate him as much as I used to."

"Still, Sammy," says Mom, "I'm sure he'd love to hear you say you actually *like* him."

"Okay. I'll tell him. But can I do it later? 'Cause right now, I'm starving."

"I bet you are," says Maddie. "Standing up to bullies is hard work."

"Yep," I say, taking a deep breath and kind of thumping my chest a little. "It's a tough job, but somebody's got to do it."

We all have a great dinner prepared by Mr. Moppenshine. In the dining room! Like I said, Maddie's doing really well these days. I guess we all are.

After dinner and homework, I decide to look in on E, who is recharging himself over in Mom's workshop.

"Thank you, E," I whisper softly. I don't want to wake him up. This is probably a weird thing to say, but he looks unbelievably happy. Especially for a robot.

I'm feeling pretty happy, too.

**CHAPTER 55**

The next morning, the alarm goes off, I wolf down breakfast with Maddie, we chat about everything, I grab my backpack, and E and I swing by Trip's house on our bikes so the three of us can race to school because we're "two-point-five minutes behind schedule" (according to E). It doesn't help that when we get to the bike rack we're mobbed by a bunch of kids who've all heard how the three of us stood up to Cooper Elliot.

In other words, I'm so super busy I never remember to tell E that I actually like him. I never let him know that he sort of feels like the big brother I sometimes secretly wish I had.

Kind of a mistake.

Because, right after school, E is late coming back to the bike rack.

That might not sound like that big of a deal, but being late for anything is extremely unusual for E since he has that built-in internal clock that syncs with the atomic clock out in Colorado, so he always knows exactly what time it is, down to the nearest yoctosecond, which, according to Mom, is equal to one septillionth of a normal second.

But E's so popular, I'm not totally surprised he's running late. He could be helping the janitor change lightbulbs again. Without a ladder. Or giving some little kids a pony ride on his shoulders.

So I wait.

For fifteen, maybe twenty minutes. Worried, I go back inside the school to look for E.

I find the janitor. He hasn't seen E.

The hallways are completely empty. So no pony rides.

I even check out the cafeteria, because sometimes E volunteers to help Mrs. Norby Rook, the head cafeteria lady, restock her shelves. Especially the heavy cans.

"I haven't seen him, hon," she tells me. "Not since lunch, when, like always, he didn't eat."

Now I'm actually starting to freak out slightly. I even check all the bathrooms, even though E never uses one unless he needs to tighten a bolt or something—then he might need the mirrors.

I look everywhere.

And I mean *everywhere*.

E is nowhere to be found. And nobody has seen him.

So I call Mom. She gets to school about one minute later.

Principal Reyes comes out to join us at the bike rack, where we all sort of stare silently at E's custom-built bike for maybe fifteen seconds.

Then Mom and Mrs. Reyes figure it out: *Somebody stole E.*

"They kidnapped him!" says Mrs. Reyes.

"No," says Mom. "They robo-napped him!"

# MISSING

## HAVE YOU SEEN THIS ROBOT?

NAME: "E"
HEIGHT: 5 FT
WEIGHT: 300 LBS
EYES: BLUE
BODY: METAL
DISPOSITION: EAGER

ANY INFO ON WHEREABOUTS, CALL **POLICE!**

**CHAPTER 56**

**M**addie and I have dinner together that night. She's totally bummed. Truth be told, I'm feeling pretty bummed, too.

"Who would kidnap E?" she wonders out loud.

"I dunno," I say with a shrug. "I guess a robot like that is worth a ton of money. Maybe some mobsters grabbed E and they're holding him for ransom."

"Wouldn't they have called?" says Maddie. "I mean, if they want ransom money, don't they sort of have to ask for it?"

She's right, of course. It's been several hours since E disappeared, and nobody's called Mom to demand money or anything else in exchange for E.

Maddie and I aren't the only ones in the house feeling down about E's robo-napping. I'm not sure how this works (or even if it's possible), but all the other robots seem sad and gloomy. Mr. Moppenshine looks more like Mr. Mope and Whine. Jimi, the electric-guitar-bot, won't play anything except the blues. Drone Malone is feeling too low to fly.

I miss E, too. Turns out he was a darn good robot. The best one Mom ever built.

# CHAPTER 57

That night it hits me: the black SUV!

The creepy car that was always tailing E and me. Maybe that SUV was from a rival robot company. Greedy people who wanted to steal all of Mom's hard work and E's secrets. Maybe some big-bucks Robotics Corp., Incorporated, scientists nabbed E at school, stuffed him into the back of that SUV, then drove him to their secret lab hidden inside a volcano somewhere so they could prod and probe E's circuits and copy his incredible moves.

This could be a case of what they call high-tech espionage.

In my school notebook, I jot down the license plate information I remember E telling me: "Indiana. Notre Dame vanity plates. AA999."

I'm about to crawl into bed and try to go to sleep (which I don't think is going to happen anytime soon, no matter how hard I try), when Mr. Moppenshine comes to my room with Hayseed.

"If there is anything we can do to help you and the municipal authorities locate and retrieve E, please do not hesitate to ask," says Moppenshine. "And please, pick up your socks."

"Whoever done did this," adds Hayseed, "why, they's meaner than a skillet full of rattlesnakes."

Now a bunch of other bots crowd into my bedroom. McFetch, Four, Scrubmarine, Blitzen, Drone Malone. They're all volunteering to do whatever they can to help bring E home.

"Look," I say, "I'll let you guys know if there's any way you can help."

"Good," says Mr. Moppenshine. "After all, Sammy, E is *our* brother, too!"

And then I have an idea.

"Drone Malone? Are you fit to fly?"

"Roger, wilco! Time for a traffic report?"

I shake my head. "Nope. You just need to find one car. A black SUV."

I show the hover-bot the license plate information. A thin green line stutters across the page. The drone is laser scanning the data, inputting it into his tracking device.

And without saying another word, Drone Malone flies through my window—which, thankfully, Mr. Moppenshine threw open about two seconds before the drone's nose cone would've cracked the glass.

# CHAPTER 58

**W**hen I go back to school after E's mysterious disappearance, Cooper Elliot jumps in my face with a vengeance.

I guess he's been thinking about his suspension, because I think he wants to suspend *me*.

From someplace high.

By my shoelaces.

Or my underwear.

"I can't decide which one I would enjoy more," he sniggers when no teachers are around to hear him sniggering. "Giving you a wedgie off a backboard in the gym or running you, upside down, up the flagpole."

"How about neither?" I say. "Can I vote for neither?"

"Nope. Not unless you have a five-hundred-pound robot with laser-beam eyeballs to protect your butt. Oh, wait. You don't. E isn't just tardy today, he's officially absent."

"Step aside, Cooper. We need to be in class. Mrs. Kunkel is probably taking attendance."

"So? You won't be in her class for long."

"Oh, really? Says who?"

"Me. Just wait, Dweebiac. I'm going to make your life at Creekside so miserable, you're going to beg your mommy to homeschool you like she homeschools your stupid little sister!"

Okay. That does it. I've had enough.

I sort of surprise myself by going nose to nose with the big jerk. I make sure my posture is ramrod stiff—just like E would have done. And then I let Cooper have it.

"You know what, Cooper? I don't need E to be my bodyguard. I can protect myself."

"Oh, yeah?"

"Yeah."

"Says who?"

"Me."

And then, E-style, I just stare at him. Hard. I do not blink. I do not breathe. I become Robo-boy.

Amazingly, this seems to confuse Cooper.

And you know what he does? He walks away.

This might be the number one reason I miss E at school: He was an excellent teacher.

# CHAPTER 59

**T**oo bad the next day at school is even worse.

Cooper Elliot is still leaving me alone. All I have to do to scare him off is stand still, bug out my eyes, and stare at him, hard. He must think Mom equipped me with deadly ray-gun contact lenses or something.

But here's what makes the day so awful: Cooper and his crew are totally harassing Trip instead. They make fun of his mismatched clothes and socks. They splash water down the front of his jeans when he's in the boys' room so everybody will think he peed his pants. During gym class, when Coach Stringer

isn't looking, they turn dodgeball into murder ball.

It gets worse during lunch.

We're back to just the two of us sitting together in the cafeteria.

I think some of our new friends want to sit with us, but they're afraid of what might happen to them if they do. Especially after they see Cooper Elliot come over and cover Trip's whole sandwich with his gigantic hand.

"You know what's better than a peanut-butter-and-banana sandwich?" Cooper sneers at Trip because, once again, there aren't any teachers around to hear him sneer.

"Um, a F-f-fluffernutter?" Trip stammers.

"Nope. A *mashed* peanut-butter-and-banana sandwich."

He leans down hard and squishes Trip's lunch into a mushy mess that's flatter than that guy Stanley.

"Heh-heh-heh," Cooper chuckles.

"Heh-heh-heh," chuckle all his cronies. Then they waltz away.

Trip looks over at me, almost hurt, as if I did something wrong.

"What?" I ask uncomfortably, which I know is a stupid question.

"Couldn't you have said something to help out? Or use your new robo-boy powers or something? Why'd you just sit there?"

"Um, I dunno." I shrug and look away. I guess it's a lot harder to stand up for someone else, without E around to back me up, than I realized.

Trip doesn't eat his sandwich. He just stares at it. It's flatter than a pancake after a steamroller rumbles over it.

We've both pretty much lost our appetites anyway.

**CHAPTER 60**

**I** 'm sorry about all this," I finally tell Trip when we're safely back in Mrs. Kunkel's classroom, where Cooper Elliot has to at least pretend that he isn't a total juvenile delinquent.

"Well," says Trip, "you should be. This is your fault. If you hadn't lost E—"

"I didn't lose him."

"Fine. You drove him away by saying all those mean things about him."

"What mean things?"

"Hmm. Let's see. Did you or did you not call E 'Error' repeatedly and to his face?"

"Yeah, but that was before—"

"And did you not state that E is 'the stupidest robot my mom ever created,' even though 'stupidest' doesn't make sense, because E is really smart?"

"Yeah, but—"

"I rest my case."

Maybe Trip is right. Maybe E wasn't kidnapped. Maybe my bro-bot ran away from home because I haven't been a very good bro.

While I'm thinking about all that, Mrs. Kunkel goes down the hall for "a quick minute" to discuss something with Principal Reyes. We're supposed to be doing silent reading.

Well, Cooper Elliot uses the quiet time to cement Trip's face to a desk. I think he used superglue, too, because it's a pretty tight seal.

Trip is beyond embarrassed. Teachers come. The

school nurse rushes in. Mr. Kressin, the janitor, brings his jumbo-sized toolbox. I'm afraid he might try to pry Trip free with a crowbar or melt the glue away with a blowtorch.

They finally set Trip free using some of Mrs. Kunkel's nail polish remover. His cheek will probably be bright pink for a day or two.

And yes, he blames me for that, too.

And you know what? I don't really blame him.

# CHAPTER 61

The next morning when we ride our bikes to school, Trip's cheek is back to its normal color and—yay—he doesn't blame me for the whole face-glued-to-the-desk thing anymore.

Yes, I did happen to bring him an extra peanut-butter-and-banana sandwich jazzed up with marsh-mallows, Reese's Pieces, and sprinkles. It's one of Mr. Moppenshine's best recipes.

IF I HAD TABASCO SAUCE, I'D ADD THAT, TOO. GIVES THE MARSHMALLOWS A KICK!

"Okay, you're forgiven, Sammy," Trip says as we pedal closer to school. "We're still second-best friends, right? Even though I said all that mean junk yesterday?"

"Definitely," I say. "Besides, a lot of what you said was kind of true. I was pretty rough on E at first. Now I'd do anything to get him back. But so far, Drone Malone hasn't been able to locate that suspicious SUV."

"Well," says Trip as we pull up to the bike rack, "looks like you guys might have some help with your investigation."

A black sedan with a swirling red light on its dashboard is parked in front of the school. A man and woman in suits—both of them wearing sunglasses, chewing toothpicks, and looking exactly like detectives on a TV cop show—climb out of the unmarked police car. When a breeze blows by, their jacket flaps flip up and I can see golden badges clipped to both their belts.

They *are* detectives. Just like on TV!

And they want to talk to a lot of kids, including me.

They want to talk to Cooper Elliot, too. They come

into the cafeteria looking for him right when Cooper is (once again) smooshing Trip's sandwich, the one with peanut butter, banana, marshmallows, Reese's Pieces, and sprinkles. It's pretty messy. Mr. Moppenshine would not be happy.

"You're buying that young man a new sandwich," says Detective Gabriel Henderson.

"Two," adds his partner, Detective Mary Jordan. "And then you're coming with us. We need to chat."

They "chatted" with teachers, too. They even chatted with Mr. Kressin, the janitor.

YOU KNOW WHAT'S REALLY A CRIME? BUBBLE GUM. UNDER THE DESKS. THE CHAIRS. YOU HAVE TO SCRAPE THE STUFF OFF WITH A CHISEL. AND DON'T GET ME STARTED ABOUT THE POWDER THEY MAKE ME SPRINKLE ON PUKE PUDDLES. WHY DOES IT SMELL LIKE PARMESAN CHEESE?

But at the end of the school day, the detectives don't arrest anybody.

(Yes, I was kind of hoping Cooper Elliot would be hauled away in chains.)

Our robo-napper is still at large.

And probably driving around in a black SUV.

CHAPTER
62

The next day, Principal Reyes calls an all-school assembly to talk about E and, while she's at it, bullying and bullies.

"Why did so many of us like E so much?" says Principal Reyes. "I have a theory: because he was strong and smart but he chose to use all that power and intelligence to do good. To make someone smile. To help Mr. Kressin change a lightbulb. To brighten students' days by helping them with their spelling.

"Of course, E could have used his incredible power to pick on anyone who was weaker than him, which, by the way, would be everybody at Creekside, including Coach Stringer. That's what bullies do. They prey on the weak. Why? Because bullies are basically cowards. They're afraid to pick on someone their own size.

"But E chose to be something better. Well, boys and girls, I want us all to be more like E. We should treat each other the way E treated us—with kindness and respect. So if you're bigger than someone, lend that smaller person a hand. If you're stronger, help them do something they couldn't do on their own. Be like E.

"If we all do that, if we treat each other the way E treated us, just think how happy he'll be when he comes back to school."

It's a very nice talk. Everybody's fired up and wants to "Be Like E."

There's only one part I don't understand: How exactly is E coming back to school if he's still missing?

# CHAPTER 63

After the assembly, some kids come over and give me pats on the back and elbow chucks.

Trip gets his fair share, too, because everybody knows we're second-best friends, so they figure E is his second-best robot friend or whatever. This one kid, a guy named Bobby Hatfield who's usually pretty nasty to me, comes over and says, "No offense," whatever that's supposed to mean.

Wait a second.

Did Bobby Hatfield robo-nap E? Was his "no offense" a confession of some kind?

Maybe it's because those detectives visited school, but all of a sudden I'm looking at everybody as if they could be suspects. Well, everybody except Trip, of course. And Principal Reyes. And Mrs. Kunkel. Actually, I don't think any of the adults did it. They all loved E, even back when I hated him.

Except, maybe, the adults riding around in that SUV.

I quickly call home. Maddie, who is monitoring Drone Malone's flights on her laptop, tells me there's still "no new news."

Then she says, "They might've taken E out of the state."

"But the SUV had Indiana tags."

"Maybe it was a rental car. Maybe they're all the way out in California. Silicon Valley."

Riding home alone on my bike, I guess I miss E more than ever.

I should've never, ever called him Error or any of those other nasty names I made up.

Maybe it really is my fault he's gone.

Yep. Trip may have forgiven me, but if E doesn't come home soon, I may never forgive myself.

Most mornings, I get up early and check on Maddie.

Then I fire up the Breakfastinator and program it to make hot cocoa (with whipped cream) and pour Cap'n Crunch for the two of us.

While that's chugging along, I dash outside and grab the newspaper for Mom and Dad. I might stop to hear what Hayseed has to say as he waters the flower beds.

But this particular morning, something interrupts my daily routine.

The first strange thing I notice on the front porch is that Dingaling, our doorbell-bot, is covered with a paper bag that totally blocks its motion detectors.

The next thing I notice is worse: three weird-looking

cardboard boxes, one on each of the porch steps.

I raise a lid and peek inside.

I can't help it. I start crying. Right there in front of the whole neighborhood.

Because E is inside the box. In pieces.

## CHAPTER 65

I go running inside, find Mom, and bring her out to the porch.

She looks at the boxes—and what is left of E. It's mostly parts and jumbled wires and bent circuit boards.

I can tell she's seriously sad.

All she says is, "I will try to fix E. If he's all here."

Dad comes out to the porch in his dragon-manga-writer bathrobe from Japan and gives Mom a big hug.

I'm kind of happy that they have each other, especially when one of them is having a horrible, awful, really bad morning. Honestly. I take back anything bad I ever said about them, now and in the future.

# CHAPTER 66

**W**ord quickly spreads around Creekside that E is back.

Well, *sort of* back.

Everybody wants to know how E is doing.

"Not great," I say, because, hey, I saw the tangled heap of loose parts and snipped wires crammed inside those three cardboard boxes.

Trip is a little more optimistic. "Sammy's mom is going to fix E," he tells everybody. "You'll see."

A lot of kids and teachers are also super supportive.

"If anyone can fix E," says Principal Reyes, "it's the

genius who created him in the first place: Professor Elizabeth Hayes, PhD. I guarantee you that, any day now, E will be back in school, *not* setting fire to anything."

Even Cooper Elliot kind of mumbles something halfway nice. "Sorry about your stupid robot, Dweebiac. You should've guarded him better."

So, okay. Not exactly the sort of sentiment you'd see inside a robot sympathy card, but I'll take it.

By the end of the day, Trip and I are getting so much attention, it's almost as if we're the most popular kids in school.

Y'KNOW, SAMMY, I MISS E AND ALL, BUT I GOTTA ADMIT—I LIKE ALL THIS ATTENTION. AND THE SWAG. THE SWAG IS **AWESOME**.

"This isn't right," I say as we're biking home.

"I know," says Trip. "We usually don't get this kind of attention. Something is definitely wrong with the universe. It's completely out of whack."

"That's not what I mean. It's not right that somebody did this to E and they're going to get away with it. We have to solve this crime."

"Um, aren't those police detectives already working on the whole 'let's solve the crime' angle?"

"Yes, but it wouldn't hurt if we gave them some help."

"Really?"

"Hey, we say the Pledge of Allegiance every morning, don't we?"

"Sure."

"Well don't forget the last part: 'with liberty and justice for all.' Well, 'all' means everybody, including E. We need to give him justice! Liberty, too!"

Yeah. I'm kind of fired up.

Plus, I have a plan: a band of bro-bots!

**CHAPTER 67**

**E**very robot Mom ever invented has some kind of special skill.

So why not use all those skills to solve this crime?

Yep. That's my big idea. Call them *RoboCops*. Or maybe this can be *CSI South Bend*, where *CSI* stands for *Cyborgs Solve It*. (Okay, I know, robots aren't really cyborgs, because cyborgs are *people* with machine implants, not machines that act like people, but it's the best I can do because I'm so busy running my brand-new robot detective bureau.)

First up is Mr. Moppenshine. Since he's so good at mopping and dusting, I ask him to dust the brown paper bag we found on the porch for fingerprints.

"Whoever placed this sack over Dingaling's motion

detectors," I say, "didn't want us to know someone was outside dropping off those boxes. If Dingaling wasn't under the bag, he would've started ringing his bell the second someone came near the porch."

"Ooh, ooh," squeals Four, the robot who acts like a four-year-old. "Maybe the bag and the boxes were put on the porch by the same person!"

(I plan on bouncing all my theories off Four first. I figure if it makes sense to a four-year-old, it'll make sense to everybody.)

"That's it!" says Trip. "You solved it, Sammy!"

"Not yet," I say, pacing around the room. "Right now, all we can say for certain is that whoever took Dingaling out of the picture had to be working with whoever made the box drop."

"I reckon the bag man come up behind Dingaling," says Hayseed. "That's why there was so many dadgum footprints in my flower beds. Looked like a squirrel stampede."

"The bag is clean," Mr. Moppenshine reports after carefully examining the brown paper sack under the microscopic eyes he uses to hunt down dust mites. "Whoever put the bag over Dingaling's eyes was wearing gloves."

"We need to look for tire tracks in the driveway," I say. "SUV tire tracks."

That's when Maddie sends me an urgent text:

Drone Malone has SUV with Indiana plate AA999. Pulling into parking garage. ND campus.

CHAPTER
68

**M**om, of course, is super busy in her workshop, trying to put E back together.

But Dad agrees to drive Trip and me over to campus, once I explain my theory.

"I think E was stolen by a rival robot engineer who wanted to steal all of Mom's secrets. They tore E apart, swiped all the information they could, and didn't bother putting E back the way they found him."

"Seriously?" says Dad.

"This same SUV parked at the end of our driveway one night," I tell him. "It followed E and me to school. It was even there when Mom and I pulled the X-14 caper to help Trip."

Dad nods. I can tell he's thinking. "We better take Blitzen. This could get dangerous."

So we load the small-but-super-strong former linebacker robot into the back of our minivan and head to the Eddy Street Commons parking garage, the structure Drone Malone saw the SUV enter. The garage is located in a shopping and dining complex right across East Angela Boulevard from the Notre Dame campus.

It's nine o'clock at night and dark out.

"Funny," says Dad as we ease up Eddy Street. "This is the garage where your mother parks sometimes. Her office in Fitzpatrick Hall is only about a ten-minute walk away."

"They came back to steal her files on E!" says Trip.

"You guys," says Dad. "Maybe we should call the police."

"We'll be okay," I say. "We have Blitzen."

I thumb the "on" button on his remote.

"I will mow them down," he says. People or grass, Blitzen's all about the mowing.

We slowly pull into the gloomy garage. Our headlights bounce up and down as our wheels roll over a speed bump.

"The bad guys probably knew Mom had a reconnaissance drone," I say. "That's why they always parked in garages instead of outdoor parking lots."

"They were sneaky," says Trip.

"Like ninjas," adds Dad.

And then we see it.

The black SUV with the ND vanity plate.

Two shadowy figures emerge from the darkness and start walking toward the parked SUV.

Both of them are carrying cardboard cartons!

# CHAPTER 69

**D**ad slams on the brakes.

I slide open the van's side door.

Blitzen rumbles out and hits the concrete running. "Blue, ninety-two! Blue, ninety-two!" I think he's calling an audible. (It's a football thing.)

Blitzen races across the oil-stained garage floor, barreling straight for the two silhouettes toting the cardboard cartons—the same kind of boxes E was packed in.

"Yikes!" shouts one of the bad guys, jumping sideways.

Blitzen keeps charging. Misses his target. Slams into a pillar. He bounces off it like a Roomba vacuum cleaner and tears across the garage, heading for another concrete column maybe twenty yards away.

He caroms off that and, like a pinball, keeps rolling across the garage floor, slamming into concrete columns and orange safety cones. I guess to Blitzen they look like tackling dummies.

I search for his remote and shut him down so that he doesn't have to go on the injured reserve list.

Meanwhile, Dad jumps out of the car and strikes one of the jujitsu poses he's always drawing for his *Hot and Sour Ninja Robots* manga books.

"Eeeyaa!" he screams.

The two shadows with the boxes freeze.

"I must warn you, my nefarious friends," says Dad, sounding like Hotsi-hiroki from his comics, "I know kung fu, karate, and several other Asian words."

He strikes his best attack pose.

The two villains suddenly relax, put their boxes down, and step into the dusty light.

"Oh, hey, Mr. Rodriguez."

"What's up?"

It's Wendy Garland and Joshua Chun. The two grad students who help Mom do all her research.

Dad turns to me. "Sammy?"

"Um, what are you guys doing here?" I ask.

"Dr. Hayes needed some of E's files that she had in her office," says Joshua Chun. "How about you guys? What are you doing here?"

"Wondering why you two were tailing E and me in that black SUV all the time," I say, still trying hard to sound like a cop on TV.

Wendy Garland shrugs. "Same old, same old. Recording data. Monitoring field results."

"Taking E to school was the final test before he could be totally certified for his ultimate real-world function," says Joshua Chun.

And E knew about the two research assistants following him around, I finally realize. That's why he did that eyebrow wiggle. He was lying when I asked him about the SUV.

"We were also monitoring his vision-action-language loop as a form of cognitive dialogue while testing the theory of real closed fields and polynomial arithmetic for motion planning," adds Wendy Garland.

Trip looks at me. I look at Dad. Dad's looking at Trip.

None of us have any idea what the egghead just said.

Only one thing's clear: These two brainiacs weren't the ones who robo-napped and then stripped down E.

So that means somebody else did.

**CHAPTER 70**

**E**arly the next morning, McFetch jumps into my bed and starts licking my face. I think Mom made his tongue out of a recycled sponge.

"What's the matter, boy?" I ask.

The robo-dog has dragged along the paper bag I found on Dingaling's head. McFetch starts sniffing it furiously and wagging his tail.

"What'd you find?"

McFetch yaps like a crazy Chihuahua—nonstop for maybe two whole minutes. Since I don't speak Chihuahua, I have absolutely no idea what McFetch is trying to say.

Fortunately, Mom equipped the robo-dog with a high-tech scent analyzer. A full-spectrum analysis report scrolls out of its snout on a tiny slip of curled paper. It's a list of everything McFetch smelled on or in the bag.

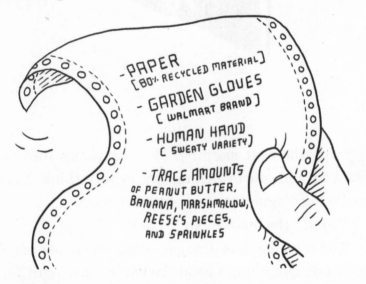

- PAPER
[80% RECYCLED MATERIAL]

- GARDEN GLOVES
[WALMART BRAND]

- HUMAN HAND
[SWEATY VARIETY]

- TRACE AMOUNTS
OF PEANUT BUTTER,
BANANA, MARSHMALLOW,
REESE'S PIECES,
AND SPRINKLES

"Wait a second," I say. "You could smell peanut butter, bananas, and all that other stuff even though the perpetrator was wearing gloves?"

McFetch yaps some more, probably to remind me that his sense of smell is about ten million times better than a human's.

I call Trip and tell him what McFetch just discovered.

"So, Trip," I ask, "do you remember what happened in school the day before I found the boxes on the front porch?"

"We had that math test?"

"And Cooper Elliot squished your sandwich in the cafeteria. The one Mr. Moppenshine made for you."

"With marshmallows, Reese's Pieces, and sprinkles!"

"Exactly. And assuming that Cooper Elliot never washes his hands because everybody tells him he *should* wash his hands, it's quite possible the sandwich stink would still be on his mitts several hours later."

"Cooper did it!"

"Or helped somebody else do it. All we need now is his confession!"

I go find Hayseed and Brittney 13.

"Come on. You two are coming to school with me today."

"Oh, goody!" gushes the always-emotional Brittney 13. She probably thinks our school has boy bands since we have a band room.

"I don't need to get all edumacated while I'm there, does I?" asks Hayseed.

"Nope. You and Brittney 13 just need to talk to Cooper Elliot."

"Talk to him? Shoot, son, I could talk a dog off a meat truck."

CHAPTER
71

Since neither Hayseed nor Brittney 13 is built for long-distance travel, Forkenstein hauls them over to Creekside for me first thing in the morning.

We corner Cooper Elliot on the playground, right near the swing set where he cornered Trip and me.

WHAT IS THIS? TAKE A HOUSEHOLD APPLIANCE TO SCHOOL DAY OR SOMETHING?

Brittney's job? She'll be our "good cop." Butter Cooper up. Get him talking. She lays it on thick.

"Excuse me, aren't you the lead singer in that awesome band?"

"Um, no…"

"Well, you sure are cute."

"You're a robot. How would you know?"

"Oh, I'm programmed to emotionally respond to cuteness. Awesomeness, too!"

"What's going on here, Dweebiac?" Cooper says to me. "Why'd you bring these two broken-down bobbleheads to school? Now that E's fallen apart, you really think these two clunkers can protect you?"

Brittney turns on the waterworks. Artificial tears spritz out of her eye sockets.

"No," she blubbers. "We want to protect *you*, Cooper Elliot. Because you're so cute. And so awesome. And so awesomely cute."

"Protect me? From what?"

That's when our "bad cop," Hayseed, moves in.

"Now then, Cooper, regardin' the disappearance of our friend E—"

"You're barking up the wrong tree."

"Is that so? Well, you know what my grandpa used to say: Don't skinny-dip with snapping turtles."

"Sammy? Turn this stupid thing off. I didn't do anything!"

"Cooper, let me tell ya—my cow died last night, so I don't need your bull."

"Huh? What's that supposed to mean?"

"Boy, you're dumber than a box of dirt if you think

we ain't got your peanut-butter-'n'-banana hands all over that paper sack."

"What paper sack?"

"The one you slipped on top of Dingaling's head to block his motion sensors."

"You mean that stupid robot thing on Dweebiac's front porch? Johnny and Trevor told me to! They said it was probably a burglar alarm."

*BA-BOOM, FA-WUMP*, and *KREEE-UNCH*! He's busted!

Cooper Elliot just confessed.

By accident!

CHAPTER
72

nother neat thing about Mom's robots?

A lot of them, including Hayseed, have digital recorders hidden inside. Hayseed now has Cooper Elliot's confession permanently stored in his memory banks.

And Brittney? Well, since Mom made her to replicate a typical teenager, she can instantly text anybody, anywhere—without a phone. It's all in her head. Plus, she's her own Wi-Fi hot spot.

So Brittney promptly texts the South Bend Police Department and suggests they send those two detectives back to Creekside.

They do.

"Thanks for all your hard work, Detectives Roboto,"
Detective Jordan says to Hayseed and Brittney 13.
Then she turns to me. "Good work, son. We'll take it
from here."

So I have Forkenstein carry Brittney 13 and
Hayseed home while I head inside to Mrs. Kunkel's
classroom, where everybody (including Mrs. Kunkel)
is standing at the window, watching the cop show
taking place out on the playground.

Then, maybe three minutes later—and this is the honest truth—the two detectives haul Cooper Elliot away in their police car!

Mom gets called down to police headquarters, too.

When I come home from school, she tells Maddie and me the whole story.

Turns out Cooper and his two knuckleheaded brothers, Johnny and Trevor, who are in the seventh and eighth grades over at Jefferson Intermediate School, were the ones who kidnapped E.

I guess they thought their "harmless prank" was hilarious. E, of course, would disagree.

From what the police told Mom, stealing E and trashing him wasn't all Cooper's idea—actually, I don't think Cooper Elliot's ever even *had* an idea— but he was definitely part of it.

Anyway, Trip and I don't have to worry about Cooper Elliot picking on us at school anymore.

Well, at least for a month.

That's how long he's been suspended this time.

# CHAPTER 73

**M**addie and I talk for a really long time that night.

I fill her in about school—as I always do—but I talk even more about E and all the amazing robots, how they worked together, and about Mom and Dad, and how I'm gaining a bunch of respect for them.

I'm feeling pretty great now that the case is closed. Maddie, too.

There's only one thing that might make both of us feel even better: having E back as our bro-bot.

For that to happen, Mom would need to do some pretty incredible surgery.

It would be kind of like putting Humpty-Dumpty back together again—only with a ton more parts and no yolk.

You could say that robots are running our entire house this weekend.

Because they do.

Why?

Because Mom's too busy over in her workshop prepping E for what she calls "brain surgery" on his main circuit board. This is the final operation that will either save E or totally erase his memory.

"If it works," Mom tells us before she disappears behind locked lab doors, "E will be E again. In fact, he might be even more remarkable. Several of his apps have upgrades available."

"And if the operation doesn't work the way you want it to?" I ask. "If you can't bring him back?"

She sighs. "Well, I guess I could construct a new robot."

"But it wouldn't be E."

"It would have the same specifications."

"But it wouldn't be E?"

"No, Sammy. It would not. E is...unique."

"Then, please, Mom, give it your all. I want my bro-bot back!"

Dad tries to keep himself busy revising *Hot and Sour Ninja Robots in Vegas*, but his head (and his heart) is over in the workshop with Mom, so he keeps making goofy mistakes. For instance, Las Vegas is *not* in Alaska. Also, people in Las Vegas do not have three eyeballs or four ears. He even gets the title wrong on the cover.

Maddie and I aren't doing much better.

She's feeling pretty good (except for her stomach, which, like mine, is filled with butterflies), so we try to pass the time in the family room playing Super Mario on the Wii U. We aren't allowed to play video games very often, so it's fun.

For almost a whole fifteen minutes.

Our minds aren't on the game. They're over in Mom's workshop.

Everybody is worried about E. Even a few of the robots are distracted.

In short, even though it lasts the usual number of hours, it's the longest weekend any of us can ever remember.

Until, finally, Mom is done!

# CHAPTER 75

**J**ust after dawn on Monday morning, Mom comes out of her workshop.

E comes out right behind her.

Well, it looks like E. But he's all jittery and kind of stumbling around and making *BZZT-BZZT, KLIK-KLIK, CHUNKA-CHUNKA* noises.

This is not good.

I guess Mom goofed up. The E I knew is gone.

I think I might start crying.

Then E wiggles his goofy eyebrows and says, "Yo—
I'm just messing with
you, bro."

"You're okay?"
I ask, goose
bumps exploding
all over my arms.

PSYCH! GOTCHA, SAMUEL HAYES-RODRIGUEZ.

"Never better, Sammy.
Kyrgyzstan. K-Y-R-G-Y-Z-S-
T-A-N. Booyah. I am defi-
nitely good to go."

His arms whirr, and his
hips swivel.

"Testing, testing. 'I thought
a thought. But the thought I thought was not the
thought I thought I thought.' All systems are up and
operational."

E fist-bumps me and does a quick little backward
moonwalk in the driveway that ends with a backflip
into a split.

"So, Sammy, did you miss me?" E asks, his eyes glowing bright blue. "I missed you for a little while and then I didn't miss you or anybody else because I was stone-cold out of it."

Mom is smiling. Dad is laughing. I've never been happier.

"I wish I could've helped you and the other bots investigate my disappearance," E continues. "However, I was unable to do so because, if I may be permitted an appropriate pun, I had fallen to pieces."

Oh, yeah. E is back—chirpier than ever. But I feel I have to tell him the whole truth and nothing but.

"I did miss you, E. Really. I did. But—and I'm just being honest here..."

"Lay it on me, bro."

"Okay. It's a little weird that you go to school with me."

"Why's that?"

"The other kids all know you're only there because Mom and Dad think I need a friend. In case you never noticed, I'm a little strange. And being strange makes it hard to make friends."

"You're not strange, Sammy. You're my brother."

"Well, isn't *that* kind of strange? Having a brother who's, you know..."

"Handsome, clever, and strong?"

"You're all that, E," I say with a smile. "But face it, you're also a robot. That's not exactly normal."

"You are correct, Sammy," says E. "I am not normal. In fact, I would daresay I am exceptionally different. I suppose strangeness is just something that runs in our family."

I look at Mom. And Dad. And E.

E's right. We're all a little different. Unique, even. *UN*usual.

And you know what? I wouldn't have it any other way.

**CHAPTER 76**

After E finishes giving me a better spin than any ride at Six Flags Great America, Mom comes over and looks me straight in the eye.

"Sammy, you're wrong. Yes, you're a little... *different*. *Good* different. But E isn't going to school because Dad and I thought you needed a new friend."

"Really?" I say.

"You can't make friends the way you make a robot. It's something you just have to do for yourself— like you did with Trip. And you'll make more. Lots more."

"That's nice of you to say, Mom, but—"

"Sammy? This is very important. So please pay attention."

"Okay."

"E is not going to school for you. In fact, Project E has absolutely, positively *nothing* to do with you at all."

"No?"

Mom shakes her head. "E is going to school for *Maddie*. And she didn't want to be the center of attention. You know Maddie….She didn't want you to worry about E's success or failure, because she knew you'd care too much. That's why I couldn't tell you what I was really trying to do."

That Maddie. She always says "it's no biggie." Of course, she knew that if I knew E had been made for her, everything he did would be a really *big* deal to me. The funny thing is how much I ended up caring about E anyway.

And now I start to realize what all this means for the future.

I remember what Mom told me back when we first talked about her new experiment.

Remember how Maddie can't go to school because of the autoimmune thing?

Well, thanks to E, all that's going to change now.

"Maddie can go to school!" I say. "Real school. E can be her eyes and ears."

Then something else hits me.

"Wait a second. Is that why E's eyes are so amazingly blue?"

Mom smiles. "Just like Maddie's."

**CHAPTER
77**

So let me tell you what happened in school later that same day.

It's actually pretty amazing.

For the first time ever, Maddie Hayes-Rodriguez is in a third-grade classroom at Creekside with other kids her age. Thanks to E's incredible HD-camera eyes and state-of-the-art audio components, Maddie gets to meet her new teacher, Ms. Tracey, the one who lets you have cupcakes on your birthday.

All of a sudden, thanks to E, Maddie has twenty-six new friends. She can hear them talk, and—get this— she can talk back to them! She can join in on classroom discussions. She can read aloud when they read aloud and solve math problems at the whiteboard and watch videos and do arts and crafts. Because E is one absolutely amazing, incredibly talented, battery-powered education machine.

It is, without a doubt, the best Monday ever at any school anywhere.

# CHAPTER 78

On Friday, after Maddie's first official full week of school, we throw this unbelievably awesome party. There's never been anything like it at our house, or South Bend, or maybe the whole state of Indiana.

Mom and Dad and I and E—and all of Mom's other crazy robots—party till the break of dawn. (We would've had the party on that amazing Monday, but it was a school night.) There are sopaipillas for everybody! And, thanks to E, Maddie gets to be there, too—without ever leaving her sterilized bedroom.

Trip comes, of course, and brings his mom. She made everybody peanut-butter-and-banana finger sandwiches.

Mom and Dad's band play some almost pretty bad music. Ms. Tracey and Mrs. Kunkel and a bunch of kids from school dance up a storm.

Turns out Mom was right about something else, too.

I *have* made a bunch of new friends at Creekside, and none of them are robots. One is even Jenny Myers!

Of course, no matter how many new friends I make, Trip will always be my second-best bud. He has dibs on that.

All the kids from school think the robots roaming around the house are the coolest things they've ever seen.

I guess they're right.

Mom's robots are pretty cool. And they all do incredibly amazing stuff.

But if you ask me, E is the coolest.

Why?

Because he's my bro-bot.

**Read on for a sneak peak**

## CHAPTER 1

## THiS IS NOT A DRiLL

Ever since I've known you—how long has it been now?—I've been getting my butt kicked in about a hundred different ways. Well, the butt-kicking officially stops here.

On this page.

Before the next period

.

That's why this could be my best story yet. I've got a ton of stuff to tell you about. More than ever, in fact. For a while, I thought maybe I'd call this book *The Butt-Kick Stops Here*. Or maybe *Look at Me, I'm Special*. Or *First Kiss*. Or *Rafe Khatchadorian: Secret Agent Artist*.

But I didn't call it any of those things. In case you haven't already noticed, I called this one *Just My Rotten Luck*.

And even though that doesn't sound like the happy-go-luckiest title you've ever heard of (with plenty of good reason), there's a lot that happens in this book that's pretty awesome.

Like me being a football hero.

Yeah, yeah. I know *football* and *Rafe Khatchadorian* don't exactly go together like ham and eggs. But that really was me, hitting the field for the Hills Village Middle School Falcons. It really did happen.

Really, really.

Don't get me wrong. I'm not saying this story is going to be all about touchdowns and cheerleaders screaming my name. (*Obviously.* I mean, have you seen what I look like?)

I'm just saying…well, you know what? Maybe I should start at the beginning. And for that to happen, we have to go back in time a little bit. And *that* means I'm going to need a good old-fashioned flashback. Then a flash-forward, and then who knows what else after that.

So buckle up, people. It's going to be a bumpy ride. All set? Good.

Here comes the flashback!

## CHAPTER 2

## ROUGH START

**W**elcome to THE PAST! Don't worry, we didn't go that far. Just three weeks earlier, to be exact.

I was at the tail end of a pretty lousy summer, which is *supposed* to be the best time of the year for most kids. Me, not so much. Camp Wannamorra had been a disaster, and my time at The Program in the Rocky Mountains just about killed me in six different ways. (Well, okay, just *one* way, but still…)

None of that was the worst part, though. That happened on the Friday before school started, when Mom took me to Hills Village Middle School. We had a meeting scheduled with Mrs. Stricker and Mrs. Stonecase so I could get re-enrolled there.

You remember Mrs. Stricker, right? And Mrs.

Stonecase too? They're the principal and vice principal of HVMS. They're also sisters—for real. That's like getting twice the trouble for half the price. Not to mention, if there was a Worldwide Khatchadorian Haters Club, they'd be the president and vice president.

So anyway, as soon as I was stuck inside that lion's den (I mean, sitting down in Mrs. Stricker's office), I got a two-ton piece of bad news dropped on my head.

"If Rafe wishes to come back to Hills Village Middle School this fall," Mrs. Stricker said to my mom, "he'll have to be enrolled as a special needs student."

And I was like, "Say WHAT?"

But Stricker wasn't done. She kept going, like a tidal wave of meanness that just couldn't be stopped. "Whether he'll finish middle school on time or have to put in an extra semester or two— or *more*—well, we just can't say at this point," she told us.

And then I was like, "Say WHAAAAAAT???"

I don't know what they call it at your school. IEP. SPED. Special Education. Barnum & Bailey's Three-Ring Circus. At HVMS, the kids have plenty of names for it—just not ones they say when any teachers are around.

And now I was in it.

I tried to talk Stricker, Stonecase, and even Mom out of making this horrible mistake, but they wouldn't budge. Mom wasn't being mean about it or anything. I know she wants what's best for me. She just said I should give it a try.

"We'll see how things go once the school year starts," she said. "Who knows, maybe you'll even like it."

Which is such a MOM thing to say.

In the meantime, if you're thinking this story is all about bad news, don't worry. Some cool stuff happens too, like that first kiss, and some other things I haven't even told you about yet.

But so far? My school year was off to the worst start ever.

And it hadn't even started yet.

## SPECiAL

Christmas is special.

Finding a dollar on the ground is special.

Personal pan pizzas with double pepperoni are special.

But getting put in a "special needs" program with "special" classes and no guarantee of getting through middle school anytime e*special*ly soon?

Not so special.

Before we left school that day, Mom and I had a meeting with my new "Learning Skills" teacher, Mr. Edward Fanucci. It's pronounced fuh-noochy, and sounds to me like something you'd eat with tomato sauce.

"Rafe, welcome back to HVMS," he said. "I'm glad we'll be working together this year. And it's

Jules, is that right, Mrs. Khatchadorian?"

"Jules is fine," Mom said.

Mr. Fanucci recognized Mom from the diner where she works—Swifty's over on Montgomery Boulevard. She even remembered that he liked his cheeseburgers well done and sat by himself at the counter for breakfast every Sunday morning.

In fact, the two of them were having a great old time talking about cheeseburgers while I sat there thinking about how miserable my life was about to get.

What did all this mean, exactly? Was I just plain dumb? Could I have gotten out of it if I'd paid more attention in school? If I'd eaten more veggies when my mom told me to? If I didn't have an imaginary friend who I used to talk to all the time?

If I wasn't so *weird*?

"Okay, Rafe," Mr. Fanucci finally said, "we need to review your IEP. Then I'll let you go, and you can start enjoying the last few days of your summer vacation."

I wanted to ask how he thought I could *enjoy* anything with this hanging over my head, but I didn't say a word. I just thought, *NONONONO NONONONO!*

Supposedly, *IEP* stands for *Individualized Education Program*. But if you ask me, it was more like *In Extreme Pain*.

Maybe I shouldn't have had that second doughnut.

I guess Mr. Fanucci could tell I was about as excited as a kid in the dentist's chair, because he started getting all buddy-buddy with me.

"Believe it or not, you're going to be glad for this program," he said. "It's going to help you do better than ever in school, like getting some extra gas in the tank. You'll take most of your classes with everyone else and work with me on your assignments. Three times a week, we'll have our Learning Skills group, with some kids like you who need extra help."

"Kids like me?" I said.

"Yeah," he said. "Kids who learn differently."

Which was just another way of saying SPECIALS. Dummies. Rejects. Weirdos. Freaks.

You know—kids like me.

## AMBUSH

**Y**ou know how I said that day was the worst part of my whole summer? Well, hold on, because the day wasn't over yet.

While Mom was talking to Mr. Fanucci some more, I asked if I could wait out in the parking lot. The last thing I wanted was for anyone to see me hanging around the office and start asking questions.

So there I was, sitting on the bumper of our car and wondering what kind of job a middle school dropout could get (answer: NONE), when my day got a little worse. And by "a little worse," I mean a *lot* worse.

"Yo! Khatcha*DORK*ian!" said a familiar voice.

I looked up and saw...wait for it...or maybe you can guess?

That's right. Miller the Killer.

Yup. Just my rotten luck.

He was coming my way, along with a bunch of guys from the HVMS flag football team. I guess they'd already started practice for the season, because they were all wearing their cleats and headed for the fields behind the school.

Which put me right in their path—like a rickety little straw hut in a hurricane.

When I first went to HVMS, Miller made my life about as enjoyable as a box of rabbit poo that you thought was juicy raisins. The last time we'd tangled, both of us ended up bloody. Mostly because he got my blood all over him.

So you could say we didn't exactly part ways as friends.

"What are *you* doing here?" Miller said. "Don't tell me you're coming back to HVMS."

"Okay," I said. "I won't tell you that."

"Wait," he said, and got that familiar, confused look on his face. "So you *are* coming back?" Miller isn't "special" like me, but he's not exactly the brightest bulb on the Christmas tree either.

"This is going to be good," Jeremy Savin said, and gave Bobby Davidson a fist bump. The way they were all looking at me, it was starting to feel like feeding time in the gorilla house at the zoo.

If I could have, I would have gotten out of there. But what was I going to do, snap my fingers and disappear? Tell him I had to go to the bathroom? (Actually, I *did* have to go to the bathroom, but that wasn't much help.)

And I couldn't tell Miller to shove it either. That would have been like sticking a piece of dynamite in my mouth and handing him a lit match.

Except then I got a lucky break. Coach Shumsky showed up at the top of the football bleachers and started yelling our way.

"Miller! Savin! Davidson!" he said. "You joining us for practice today? Or are you planning on sitting out the opening game this season?"

"Coming, Coach!" Jeremy called.

"Right away, Coach!" Miller said, like they were in the army or something. Trust me when I tell you, these guys take their flag football verrrrrry seriously. Once they get into high school, they'll play full tackle ball. In the meantime, they like to practice their tackling skills on guys like me.

"This isn't over," Miller told me, and pointed a finger right in my face. I could even smell what he'd had for lunch: bologna sandwich, spicy mustard, and grape soda.

"*What's* not over?" I said. "There's nothing… started."

That's when he gave me one of his Miller-sized chest thumps. If I hadn't been shoved up against Mom's bumper, I probably would have fallen flat on my butt. And it wouldn't have been the first time.

"*Now* it's started," he said. Then he and his gorilla goons headed off toward the field.

To be honest, I've never understood why Miller hates me so much. The only reason I hate him is because…well, because he hates me. I know I should have kept my mouth shut at that point. Obviously. But I'm not always so good at *should*.

"Hey, Miller!" I said. "What's your problem, anyway? What have you got against me?"

Miller just looked back at me once, shrugged, and kept on walking.

"Soon as I remember, you'll be the first to know," he said. "See you in school, buttwipe."

Yeah. That's exactly what I was afraid of.

**JAMES PATTERSON** is the internationally bestselling author of the highly praised Middle School books, *Homeroom Diaries*, *House of Robots*, *Kenny Wright: Superhero* and the I Funny, Treasure Hunters, Maximum Ride, Confessions, Witch & Wizard and Daniel X series. James Patterson has been the most borrowed author in UK libraries for the past eight years in a row and his books have sold more than 300 million copies worldwide, making him one of the bestselling authors of all time. He lives in Florida.

**CHRIS GRABENSTEIN** is a *New York Times* bestselling author who has also collaborated with James Patterson on the I Funny and Treasure Hunters series. He lives in New York City.

**JULIANA NEUFELD** is an award-winning illustrator whose drawings can be found in books, on album covers, and in nooks and crannies throughout the Internet. She lives in Toronto.